Gently with the millions

A man who is reputed to have scribbled six-figure cheques without even breaking sweat, Charles Reason was once Managing Director of a respected City firm. Now, at Big Bang, the business has been merged with a Swiss bank, and Reason, suspected of insider-dealing, is a disgraced man, lucky to have avoided prosecution.

A widower, he lives alone, his battered Mini hemmed in by Porches and BMWs, a sad sign of his reduced circumstances. However, the neighbours' gossip soon excites the sympathy of Chief Superintendent George Gently's wife, Gabrielle, and a drama of classic proportions begins to unfold.

Yet Gently smells a rat at Reason's affectation of riches turned to rags. And when a locked room in the ex-tycoon's flat is discovered to contain a battery of computer screens and six telephones, his suspicions are confirmed.

As the news gets out, the 'vultures' descend: Reason's daughters, Olivia and Susan (traduced by their father respectively as 'She-wolf' and 'Jezebel') and the beloved Ginny, whose sudden death sets off a murder enquiry which only the experienced Gently, pursuing his thirty-seventh investigation, can hope to bring to a satisfactory conclusion.

Other murder cases investigated
by Chief Superintendent Gently, CID.

GENTLY WITH THE MILLIONS

Alan Hunter

Constable London

First published in Great Britain 1989
by Constable & Company Limited
10 Orange Street, London WC2H 7EG
Copyright © 1989 by Alan Hunter
Set in Linotron 10pt Palatino by
Centracet, Cambridge
Printed in Great Britain by
St Edmundsbury Press Limited
Bury St Edmunds, Suffolk

British Library CIP data
Hunter, Alan, *1922–*
Gently with the millions
I. Title
823'.914 [F]

ISBN 0 09 469440 0

The characters and events in this book are
fictitious; the locale is sketched from life.

In memory of my sister
AUDREY HELEN BENNETT

1

And as we dropped him at his flat with his battered suitcase, covered with the rubbed stickers of some very good hotels, he paused briefly, his watery grey-blue eyes seeking mine.

'Are you into equities at all?'

'Well – yes. A modest investment.'

'Sell the buggers. What happened in August was more than a correction.'

Then he'd nodded to Gabrielle and slunk away into the flat.

Gabrielle said: 'Will you take his advice?'

I shook my head. 'I'll think about it.'

And in the end I did sell, against the clamorous persuasions of my broker; a fortnight to the day before the dawning of Black Monday.

It was two months earlier when the rusted Mini had first appeared in Lime Walk, and initially I had supposed it to be the property of someone's daily help. But it was still there in the evening, hemmed in with Porsches and BMWs, and remained planted there all week, gathering dust and falling leaf. My policeman's instincts were aroused. I took the trouble to inspect the licence. The licence had ten months yet to run and had been issued at the local post-office in Kensington. The tyres were good, and the rust, though widespread, apparently superficial; on the back seat lay a week-old *Financial Times*, folded back at the share-price listing. I queried Gabrielle.

'Have you seen who it is that belongs to the Mini?'

'No, my dear. But I mean to find out. There is certainly a new tenant in that ground-floor flat.'

Since we took up residence in Lime Walk Gabrielle has formed a wide acquaintance there, and is usually abreast of the gossip that goes the yuppie rounds in Holland Park and Kensington. Two days later she'd struck pay-dirt.

'My dear, he's a bust broker.'

'A what?'

Gabrielle giggled. 'That's what Julie Mannering calls him. She shares the same Mrs Mop, but better than that, she knows his daughter. And this daughter, would you believe, is married to a New York millionaire, while he has two other well-off daughters, one of whom lives in Belgravia.'

'But he's . . . bust?'

'Oh yes. A little more than bust, Julie thinks. There was this, what you call, Big Bang, ha? When all the rules were changed in the city. Then his firm is taken over by a bank, and funny things are coming to light. It seems, he is lucky to have escaped a prosecution, and certain it is he lost every penny. Julie thinks the daughters pay his rent and pay him also a small remittance, but for the rest do not wish to know him. He has blotted his book, yes?'

'What's his name?'

'Charlie Reason.'

It meant nothing to me.

'Have you seen him?'

'But yes. This morning. And he matches his little car, my friend. An old man in a shabby coat with grey hair down to his shoulders, he is coming out of the house when I am returning from Julia's. So, why not, I say

8

"Good-morning, Mr Reason!" – and he stops to stare with his hazy eyes. Then he touches the old hat he is wearing, and that is that, we go on our ways. But there is more mystery too about this man. In the flat is a room which he keeps always locked. Once, the cleaner asks him for the key, and he flies in a rage – she must not enter there!'

'Just his souvenir room, perhaps.'

'Aha. Is what you say.'

'Has he no wife?'

'She is dead several years. One must feel sorry for this man, I think.'

Next day at the Yard I mentioned Reason's name to a colleague in the Fraud Squad.

'Charles Sinjohn Reason? Ye-es. So that's where the poor old sod has got to.'

'Is he known to us?'

'Not really. Just some murky rumours going around. He was managing director of Haarz-Reason-Webb which merged with Credit Zurich at Big Bang. Rumour was he'd siphoned off a fair chunk and had to make restitution pretty sharpish – Rolls, yacht, villa, house in Belgravia all went down the drain. Rags to riches, riches to rags. You see it all in this job.'

'But I understand his children are quite well-off.'

'The youngest married a DeWitt of DeWitt-Oppenheimer. Another is the wife of a merchant banker. I can't think they're overjoyed by daddy's exploits.'

Probably not. But one couldn't help feeling that a little more support might have been forthcoming. When I saw him, I found it difficult to imagine that this trampish old man had once been among the millions. Always he wore the same shabby coat, bundled about his heavy figure, the same stained homburg, down-at-heel shoes. And nestled in untidy grey locks, a large-featured, reddened countenance, with prominent nose, prominent brows and watery, evasive blue-grey eyes. A man who greeted no

9

one, who was despised by his yuppie neighbours. Whose 'seventies Mini was invariably blocked in by a Merc ahead and an Audi astern.

And who I found drinking tea in our flat with Gabrielle when I returned one afternoon.

He put down his cup, rose, but didn't seem to know if he should offer his hand. I took it anyway. Gabrielle said:

'George, this you simply will not believe. Mr Reason knows our house, Heatherings, and stayed there when Colonel Jonson had it. A coincidence, yes?'

Yes indeed. Reason's look was a little sheepish. He said casually:

'The Festival and that, I was often up there in the old days. Knew Jonson, pal of my son-in-law's. That's the one who lives in Yonkers.'

'You came up for the Festival?'

'In my wife's time. I haven't been back there since. Once I had a mind to buy Jonson's house, but then – ' He shrugged. 'Things change.'

He spoke with a low, apologetic voice, but the watery eyes met mine firmly. Divested of the coat, he was wearing a well-cut lounge suit, but the cut was of a decade earlier. He said:

'I suppose you've heard the tale?'

'I've heard you've suffered some reverses.'

He grunted. 'That's a kind way of putting it! But maybe I was getting tired of money, anyway. That happens, believe me. You have to have had money to know the truth. It buys trash, just trash. And in the end it's a disease.'

I said: 'But handy, though.'

'Oh, it buys shelter, food, transport. But after that it wastes a man, begins to take away his meaning.'

He was sitting again now, and Gabrielle had poured me

10

tea. I sat opposite him. He was leaning forward, staring through his dishevelled locks.

'You've never had money, have you? I mean after the first million?'

'Not even that!'

'Then listen to a man who has been there and come back. There comes a point, and it's easily reached, when the damned stuff starts to get away from you. You try to spend it, but each time what you buy just turns to more gold.'

'It sounds quite a trick.'

'No – listen. I bought myself an executive jet. So sometimes it was unserviceable, and I bought myself another. Now I had two, which meant that one spent most of its life sitting in its hangar – until an airline wanted to borrow it, when suddenly I was in the charter business.'

'But that was a one-off affair – '

He shook his head. 'It happened again. I bought a yacht. Same thing. A country house. Almost at once, someone wanted it for a conference centre. And with straight investment it's worse. You feed a programme into a computer. Then the stuff starts racing away until it only makes sense to another computer. And all the time you're living in the real world with children, sickness, grief, a world you can't spend your way out of. That's on the far side of the million.'

I shook my head too. 'Then you don't regret having gone bust?'

He looked away. 'I should have chosen it. Being skint is like a breath of fresh air.'

'Just a few hundred thou?'

'Don't taunt me,' he said. 'I've got my roof, and even a car. To you it may not seem much. For me, it's all I need just now.'

'You have your children,' Gabrielle said.

11

Reason said nothing. Then he rose. 'I'm being a nuisance – I'd better go! I'm sure your husband is wanting a meal.'

'Wait,' Gabrielle said. She glanced at me. 'On Friday, we go to Heatherings. You shall come with us, Mr Reason. The Suffolk air will do you good.'

'Oh, you don't want me.'

'But yes. You are telling me you know the Festival people – our good Doctor Capel and his quintet, and Walter Hozeley, and Lady Luce.'

His hand went to his face. 'Please. I was last up that way with Marie. I swore I'd never go back to Suffolk. I think to see it now would break my heart.'

'Oh, you poor man!' Gabrielle jumped up and put her arm round his shoulders. 'But you will come. You will come with us. With friends who understand your grieving. It is best. There should not be a place where grief will not let you go.'

'Please. Please.'

'Yes – you will come!'

He pushed her away, staring wildly. Then he touched her eager face, saying: 'And you, you are not a daughter of mine!'

I helped him on with the old coat, put the stained homburg in his hand. When he had gone. Gabrielle said fiercely: 'I think those children have much to answer for.'

'You think they neglect him?'

'Aha. I have all the dirt from Julie. The eldest is married to a rich banker, the youngest to a Yankee millionaire, while the third was married to a property developer and lives now on a fat allowance. And they despise their father, ha? They let him live in old clothes? Cannot visit him in his poverty, and comfort his grief for his lost wife?'

'The locked room,' I said.

'But yes. Locked in there all his memories of her.'

'He's certainly a character.'

12

'Better he deserves. Only let those daughters of his stay away from me.'

And she was a good deal silent that evening, staring at the television with distant eyes.

And Reason did come with us.

On the Friday evening he turned up at our door with the battered suitcase and wearing, surprisingly, a coat less old, a homburg unstained, and a pair of shoes that were quite presentable.

'If you're sure it doesn't upset any plans . . . ?'

He rode behind us in the Rover. Gabrielle had music playing softly on the radio and talked to him gaily over her shoulder. He seemed in fair spirits. It was the end of summer, and we drove through darkness for most of the way; nevertheless, he grew silent as we approached our beloved Heatherings. Then:

'Which bedroom am I to have?'

'Monsieur may have the choice of three,' Gabrielle laughed. 'But, for myself, I would choose the White Room, which has a fine view across the Walks.'

'Not the White Room.'

'No?'

'I don't think I could sleep there.'

'Oh monsieur, it has been redecorated and refurnished but last year.'

'It is still the same room.'

'Then, as you wish.'

'Perhaps I'd better have a room at the inn.'

But he slept at Heatherings and, in the morning, went for a long stroll over the Walks, where there was still a hue in the ling and the mountain ashes were gay with berries. He seemed happier when he returned. He had met no one, he told us; it had been good to find the place unchanged, and almost as though he had never been away. And then, hesitatingly:

'It was seven years back. Poor Marie couldn't make the walk that day. Ginny was with me. She's the best one. I haven't had the heart to tell her what's happened.'

'You mean she doesn't know?' Gabrielle exclaimed.

'No. Unless the other two bitches have told her. They may have done, just to upset her. But I think she would have been across here.'

'Is she the one in New York?' I asked.

'Yes. Ginny. She's my youngest. The one most like poor Marie. Heaven knows who the other two take after. But Ginny's kind. It would break her heart if she saw the way I'm living now. The last time she was over I had the Rolls waiting, carried her off to my spread in Wiltshire.'

'But,' Gabrielle said, 'should she not know? Is it quite fair to keep this from her?'

He shook his head. 'Not quite yet. I can't bear to. Ginny loves me.'

Silence for a moment!

I said: 'But your other children know of your plight. I understand they are comfortably off and well able to offer you assistance.'

'Oh no.' His expression had hardened: and suddenly his eye was missing mine.

'But you need help if you're flat broke. Remember, we know what the rents are in Lime Walk. And even a modest car costs. Don't they contribute . . . just the basics?'

'Not a penny! And I'd never ask them.'

'Then . . . ?'

Angrily he tossed his grey locks. 'I can get by. I still have a little. It may not be much, but it's enough. It covers the rent and the car and all the food an old man eats.' The wild look came into his eyes. 'And who knows? The old

14

man may not be beaten yet. Give me the price of that car out there and I could make rich men of the pair of us.'

'You'd still play the markets?'

'I'm not senile yet. What I did once I can do again. Only nothing ever came of nothing. You need a stake to begin the game.'

'A loan from your children?'

'Never!'

'Oh monsieur,' Gabrielle said, 'you must think of the future. You cannot for ever be living on a shoe-string, and at last your children may not be so unkind.'

'I've done with them. Except Ginny.'

'It is just now you are thinking this.'

He shook his head and went on shaking it, anger in his eyes, in the set of his mouth.

'It's my own fault. I know that. Nothing they wanted but they had it. For me, it was a luxury to spend the money, to buy some trash that had a meaning. Clothes. Cars. Houses. Jewels. They asked, they had, from the cradle up. Poor Marie chided me, and I didn't listen. And so, and so. It comes to this.' He was breathing faster. 'Daddy is broke. It's going the rounds that he sailed too close. He's had to sell up, make himself scarce, perhaps be lucky that he's still around. That was the test, eh? The test of his loving daughters. The test I put upon them. And the test that they failed.'

I said: 'The test . . . ?'

'Yes – the test! The test of poverty and ill repute. I made sure they knew where I had moved to, but not one nor other has been near since. Olivia let it be known that I wouldn't be welcome at her house. And Susan flew off to Cannes, where she's probably staying yet. That leaves Ginny, my Ginny. Who I haven't yet dared to tell.'

It was moving, it had to be moving . . . and yet, I was shaking my head, too. Something about this man was puzzling me, something that rang only partly true. What?

15

His grief was genuine, and his anger with his children, while my colleague at the Yard had confirmed that his honesty was barely suspect. He had sailed close: but he'd paid his dues. Many in the City had done the same. And now he was skint, or nearly so, and wearing old clothes from his years of affluence. A moving figure. Except . . . ? There was something I couldn't put my finger on.

'It is too soon,' Gabrielle said. 'For you, for your daughters, this great shock. It will get better. They will understand. Is it not their father these things have happened to?'

He gazed from under his grizzled brows, his rheumy eyes pitying.

'You haven't met them. Pray God you don't. They belong to a different world to yours.'

'But still daughters, yes?'

'I call them mine. And poor Marie wouldn't have played me false. But the test came, and they failed it. Why should I call them daughters of mine?'

'Monsieur, you are too bitter!'

'They have made me eat bitter bread.'

'You are yet in shock from such losses.'

He stared at her still. But said no more.

In the afternoon he drove with us to Shinglebourne, and there we saw a different side of Reason. Our friend Capel, of course, knew nothing of his descent from riches to rags. He was welcomed like a revered uncle, both by the Doctor and by Tanya, his wife, kissed by the latter, patted by the former, and sat down with a whisky and a whopping cigar. He seemed pleased. At once they were launched into talk of festivals and music, of Hozeley's River concerto, the prospects of grabbing the Phil next year. And slowly Reason unthawed, began to chat with sparkling eye, gave a very shrewd opinion of the concerto

16

and quoted, off hand, a figure for the Phil. And suddenly the man in the 'seventies lounge suit had acquired a new authority. Now it was the Festival Maecenas who was sitting there behind the cigar. Gabrielle nudged me.

'Can it be the whisky?'

'So far, he's only had three fingers.'

'It is, perhaps, his first for some time.'

'Well, it's certainly worked the oracle.'

Reason was in deep discussion with Tanya when Capel quietly rose, and nodded to me. I followed him through to his pleasant study with its yacht half-model and stone circle photographs.

'You old devil – springing Charlie on us! I thought we'd seen the back of him for good. He dropped out when he lost his wife, you know. And now, at the psychological moment – !'

'I wouldn't expect too much.'

'Oh, it'll only be peanuts to him. You heard the fee he suggested for the Phil . . . well, would you say the time was ripe?'

'I think you've wasted your cigar.'

'Go on. Old Charlie's a second Croesus.'

'He's broke.'

'Pull the other one.'

'Scuppered. Stymied. Snookered. Broke.'

'I'm not hearing you.'

'But it's the truth. Not a Rolls left to his name.'

It took me a long time to convince him, and then his long face was solemn.

'The poor old devil. My, I'm glad I asked you before I started in back there. Not a bean?'

'About one bean. Enough for a roof and a beat-up Mini.'

'But what about his family?'

'They've given him the shoulder. Except the one in New York, who doesn't yet know.'

'Good God.' Capel pushed aside papers, sat himself on

17

the edge of his desk. 'And he's a man who'd scribble six-figure cheques without even breaking sweat. You're sure it's true?'

'As sure as I can be.'

'He godfathered the Festival, you know. It would never have got off the ground if Colonel Jonson hadn't fetched him here. He met Hozeley, talked it over, slapped his cheque-book on the table. And every season, till his wife died, he was ready to pick up the tab. After that we felt the draught, I can tell you, until the local brewers kicked in.'

'Did you meet the daughters?'

'Of course.'

'What was your impression of them?'

'Pretty flash. At least, the eldest one, a tall, rangy animal with long chestnut hair and dangling ear-rings. She was married to Fred Welles, a decent cove, a director in someone's bank. The second one was a freckled filly, always trying to outshine her sister. She hooked Rollo Strickland for a season, then got demoted and put on the pay-roll. We see life, you know, here in Shinglebourne.'

'And the youngest girl?'

'Ah. She was the quiet one. I never knew quite what to make of her, she was usually trailing about with her parents.'

'She married an American.'

Capel nodded. 'A Wall Street cowboy, one Jason DeWitt. He was worth the other two several times put together, which didn't endear her to her loving sisters. And you say she doesn't know that her dadda is bust?'

'Reason hasn't had the heart to tell her.'

Capel stared. 'Well, she'll have to know some time, and my feeling is the sooner the better. If anyone is going to stand by Charlie, I'd back his little daughter Virginia DeWitt.'

'He may be too proud to ask.'

18

'Tchah.'

'He seems to have a special feeling for her.'

'So much the better. And, in any case, it's only asking a dividend on what he's invested.'

We had left a lounge that was buzzing, but returned to a lounge that was silent. Gabrielle, Tanya, were looking apprehensive; Reason's scowling eyes were fixed on us. He snapped at Capel:

'So he told you, did he?'

'Look, Charlie old lad, I'd no idea – '

'That's the Phil gone up the spout, isn't it? Unless your brewer's pocket is deeper than I think it is.'

'Charlie, believe me!'

'And, for the record, I had another scotch while you were out – put it down to past favours. Or, if you like, I've still got the price of a dram somewhere.'

Capel was wringing his great hands. 'Charlie, for God's sake don't talk like that! You're among friends, Charlie. We don't care whether you're solvent or skint.'

'But you were going to touch me for the Phil, weren't you?'

'All right – but what's the harm in that? In the old days you'd have jumped at it, said it helped you out with your tax.'

'While now I'm a broken reed.'

'Oh, for crying out!'

'Scrounging a weekend with your friends.'

'Oh Lord, George, you talk to him. Losing his pelf must have turned his brain.'

Reason glared from under his brows. 'I wouldn't write me off yet, doctor. It's still all here, still with me, I could go into the market tomorrow. A ride with Futures, eh, then a raid in the Unlisted. Oh yes. Give me a stake, and I can still have Phils coming out of my ears.'

'Charlie, it doesn't *matter*.

'What's the price of scotch?'

19

'Charlie, you'll break my bloody heart.'

He simmered down. He let Capel talk to him: let Capel make his peace. But what bothered me about that little spat was that I could sense that Reason was enjoying it. He had got his man wrong-footed and was deliberately laying it on. As though he was finding in his poverty a weapon that he delighted in putting to use. Once more I was puzzled. On the drive back to Heatherings I had a cautious word with him.

'You were a little hard on Henry.'

In my mirror, I could see a malicious grin on Reason's face.

'He was shocked too. And you couldn't blame him for trying to push the fortunes of the Festival.'

'So he passed the test.'

Again that word!

'Was there any need to test him?'

'Where money is concerned. I've been testing you too, George Gently.'

'Me!'

In the mirror, the malicious eyes had found mine.

'What would it take to buy Heatherings?'

'You know very well that it isn't for sale.'

'That's why I'm asking. What would it take? Let's start the bidding at half a big one.'

'Monsieur Reason,' Gabrielle said, 'no money in the world will buy our Heatherings. It is a house and more than a house. It is the structure of both our lives.'

'A million?'

'Not ten million.'

'Start thinking about it,' Reason said. 'You could build such another house brick for brick, and only scratch the first million.'

'Then we have lost what the money cannot buy.'

'The one house exactly like the other.'

'But no. It has not our sky, our Walks, the little green

butterflies that come in May. And not our dear, dear house, but a ghost, an illusion.'

'Twenty million.'

'No. No.'

'Your husband drives. He says nothing.'

'He has nothing to say.'

'Twenty-five million.'

'I think it is true,' Gabrielle said, 'what you were saying before, that money in the end becomes a disease.'

'Yet, if I could still have backed that bid?'

'Also, that the good doctor's whisky talks.'

He chortled to himself. Had we passed the test? The rest of that drive passed in silence.

The next morning he failed to appear punctually at breakfast, and we sent Mrs Jarvis to root him out. She returned alone, with an expression of pity on her homely cockney face.

'Where is he?'

'In the White Room, Mr George. I didn't dare to disturb him. Standing there by the window, he is, with the tears running down his poor old cheeks. And he's got a photograph in his hands, a picture of a woman. His missus, I'd say.'

'Serve breakfast.'

'Right you are. But it give me a turn, seeing him there.'

He joined us twenty minutes later, but made no mention of his vigil in the White Room. The day was fine; we drove to Walderness, picnicked on the dunes, called on the Reymerstons. Was the visit doing him good, or harm? At times, he seemed almost bored with us. Then, again, I caught him watching us with a glint in his eye, as though some mischievous thought were stirring in his brain. An uneasy guest; I wasn't sorry when the long weekend was over, when I turned the Rover into Lime Walk and paused to set him down at his doorstep.

'Sell the buggers.'

Yes, I sold them, was completely liquid when the crash came. I would like to have thanked the lonely old man. But he wasn't around just then.

2

There followed a hectic few days in pursuit of a killer who sought his victims at railway stations, and I had small time to bother my head about bust stockbrokers and their families. The Mini caught my eye daily as I hastened round to the mews to collect my car, but just as often I blanked it from my mind and returned my attention to where it belonged. I didn't *want* to think about Reason. I felt sure that, in some way, he was playing a part. What it was I couldn't guess, and that made me feel a resentment towards him. So I frowned at the Mini and forgot it. And kept my mind on trapping criminals.

But if I forgot him, Gabrielle didn't; I think she saw him every day, and on the Thursday she met me at the door in a sort of anxious flutter.

'My dear, I have talked to Julie. And, together, we have taken a decision.'

'A decision . . . ?'

'Aha. Tonight, she shall ring Charlie's daughter in New York.'

'Oh dear!'

'You do not like?'

'I think that Reason may not like.'

'But, my dear, before long she must learn the truth anyway, and will it not be best that she should hear it from a friend?'

23

We went inside. There was fresh-made tea, and she hastened to pour me a cup; I took it to the bay window, from which I could see the rusty little car parked just down the pavement.

'So . . . ?'

'Isn't it possible that he's afraid to tell his daughter – afraid, because she's his favourite, and he fears she may react like her sisters?'

'Oh, but she isn't like her sisters!'

'You have only your friend's word for that.'

'But yes, Julie is at school with her, and, later on, at university. Also, Julie has met the husband, a man who has always admired Charlie. And it is true, Ginny loves her father, will not see him living like this.'

'But will his pride allow him to accept their help?'

'Aha, this is thought of too. You are forgetting that Charlie is a brilliant man who knows the stock markets back to front. Not now so good over here, ha? Over here, they think he has been too smart. But over there, another matter, and such a man is worth a golden hallo.'

'You think they'll offer him a job?'

'Is quite certain. Her husband is big in his family firm. Before now it is a suggestion that Charlie should join them in New York. They have a big house in this place, Yonkers, with lots of room for Charlie too, and there he will live with his good daughter while, with the husband, he plans the big coups. Is it not the solution?'

'I suppose it . . . could be.'

'Then do not be shaking your head, my friend!'

'Just, that if it's all so easy, it would probably have happened by now in any case.'

'Oh yes, and his pride, you were saying! Is that not the obstacle, until now? It has not happened because he needs the push, will not be first to play a card.'

I stared at the Mini. 'We don't know this man. There may be more to him than meets the eye. I would sooner we didn't get involved in this, left affairs to take their course.'

'But – what is it we do not know?'

I shrugged: that was the question! 'Just that he's a very unusual man, with a very unusual background.'

'But Julie knows all. She knows the family. Over many years she has known this man. He is just old, and poor, and grieving over his children and a wife beloved. What more to know, and what better to do than to help him back to wealth and affection? I think you are over-cautious, my friend. There is nothing but good can come of this.'

'Your Julie is determined to take this step?'

'She rings tonight. Which is day over there.'

'Then let us hope she knows what she is doing.'

'Oh, pouf! And you have not yet given me a kiss.'

Julie, apparently, made that call, but there was no sudden explosion on Friday. Gabrielle, who was certainly keeping an eye on Reason's flat, had nothing to report when I returned home. He hadn't even been out, it appeared; and she had not yet ventured to ring his doorbell. A thoughtful Gabrielle that evening! And I was still wishing she'd played no part in it.

This was the weekend when I was on call and which we were obliged to spend at the flat. I needed to go in for morning conference, but I was back at the flat before noon. Once more Gabrielle was waiting at the door, and this time her hazel eyes were bright with excitement.

'My dear – she's here!'

'His daughter . . . ?'

'But yes. She arrived by taxi an hour ago. And listen, he rang upon the phone, and wishes us to join them as soon as you are back.'

'Did he say why?'

'No. But he is not angry, that I can tell. He sounded happy and in a great hurry, and I am hearing her voice in the background.'

'But why want to see us?'

'I cannot say. Unless he wishes to share his joy with his friends.'

I wanted to think about it for a moment, but Gabrielle was tugging at my arm. So we made our way round to his flat, to find the front door already open.

'Come in – come in!'

He'd seen us arrive, and was beckoning from a doorway down the passage. We entered a very presentable lounge that was smelling both of cigar-smoke and of scotch. The cigar was in Reason's hand; his flushed face was grinning at us from among the grey locks. Seated on a divan was a slim, fair-haired girl, dressed in a smart two-piece and a lacy blouse. Reason waved the cigar.

'So what do you think of her?'

'Oh, madame!' Gabrielle exclaimed, darting forward to take her hand. 'So you are the person we have heard so much of – and arrived here so soon, like a good fairy!'

'Took the evening flight,' Reason said. 'You wouldn't think it to look at her, would you?'

'Poor madame must be weary to death.'

The girl made a face. 'I know I've lost some sleep.'

'Well, you'll make up for that, girl,' Reason said. 'I've booked you a room at Bertie's Hotel. But what do you think of her, George Gently, this daughter of mine, Virginia DeWitt?'

I took her hand too, and got a warm smile from eyes that were grey-blue, like her father's. She had rather fey features, straight-nosed, fine-boned, and wore on the blouse a crescent brooch set with emeralds and diamonds. By her lay a lizard-skin handbag; in the hall I'd noticed a pig-skin suitcase.

'Daddy tells me you are good friends who invited him

26

to Heatherings last weekend. That's a sure way to his heart. All of us have stayed there and loved that house.'

'And I'm told I have to thank you,' Reason said, grinning at Gabrielle, 'for Ginny's turning up here today – you, and that busybody Julia Mannering, who's always poking her finger into other people's affairs.'

'Oh Monsieur Charles, forgive me!' Gabrielle cried. 'But you are seeming so unhappy and so alone. And you are telling us of one person who is so dear to you – should we not give her, at least, a hint?'

'Ah well, ah well!' Reason patted her shoulder. 'Now she's right here in Lime Walk. And see what she has brought with her from that good-looking husband of hers.'

He picked up a letter and handed it to me. It was written on paper with an address printed in gilt. In brief, it said that Reason now being a free man, a directorship was waiting for him at DeWitt-Oppenheimer, signed Jason Carey DeWitt. I showed it to Gabrielle, who exclaimed in delight.

'Handsome, isn't it?' Reason chuckled. 'These Americans don't beat about. When they have a favour to do, they come right out with it.'

'Oh daddy, it's you who are doing the favour,' Virginia DeWitt said. 'Jason has wanted to grab you for ever. He says that with you on the board they can really get stuck into Europe.'

Reason looked at her slyly. 'Did he quote figures?'

'Yes, and you're not going to quarrel with those! You'll be among the best-paid men on Wall Street, and of course there's an honorarium.' She reached for her bag. 'I've brought a cheque – '

'Never mind, never mind,' Reason said. 'Just testing. I know Jason. We'll take the small print as read. And where am I living?'

'With us, of course.'

27

'You won't want me under your feet.'

'Oh daddy, that house is vast, you can have the whole east wing to yourself – your own domestic staff, if you like, and your own kitchen, everything. It's much too big for us, even if I had a dozen children. The nuisance will be that I shall probably never see you unless we make appointments to meet.'

Reason sighed. 'Can you beat it?' he said. 'They'd have me be an instant millionaire. Just when I thought I'd done with all that, had shaken the dust of it off my feet.'

'Daddy, you talk nonsense!'

'Do I?'

'Monsieur Charles, this is spendid!' Gabrielle said. 'Now it is the dust of Lime Walk you are shaking off, and all the sad life you have been living here.'

'Oh, we'll make up for it,' Virginia DeWitt said. 'Daddy, you're coming back with me. It's all arranged. We fly back next week. We're going to make you forget this horrid time.'

Reason turned to me. 'What do you say, George Gently?'

I shrugged. 'I think you are a lucky man.'

'You'd do what she says? Fly off to America?'

I stared at him: said nothing. And he began to laugh, great throaty peals, his watery eyes creased up with mirth. He threw the cigar into a bowl and held his sides with crowing laughter. It was almost frightening. His poor daughter had jumped up and was staring at him in dismay.

'Daddy – oh daddy!'

'Ah – ha-ha!'

'Daddy, stop it! Daddy, what's wrong?'

'Nothing wrong, little mouse – ha, ha!'

'Then daddy – please!'

'Oh dear. Oh dear.'

He controlled himself at last, except for odd rumbles

that kept breaking out. Then he took his daughter by the shoulders, smoothed the hair from her brow, gazed into her eyes.

'Then you still love me, little blossom?'

'Love you? Of course I love you!'

'You wouldn't turn your back like some people, and let your poor old father starve?'

'Daddy, how can you say that!'

'Oh, I can say it, little girl. And you won't take amiss what I'm going to say to you now?'

'Nothing – nothing.'

'Then it's this. I won't be coming back to New York. I won't be accepting Jason's offer. I won't be living in a wing in Yonkers.'

'But daddy – you must!'

He made the grey locks swirl.

'Yes, you're coming! I won't not let you.'

'Monsieur, you break her heart,' Gabrielle said. 'Do not pretend you are not going.'

His eye found mine. 'And you, George Gently?'

I went on staring and saying nothing.

'Ha, ha!' Reason chortled. 'The policeman is cautious. He smells a rat.'

'Daddy . . . what's wrong?'

'Nothing, little truepenny. Nothing at all. Everything's right, and God's in his heaven. Come this way, and I'll show you all.'

He kissed her, patted her arm, then led us out into the hall. At the far end was a heavy panelled door fitted, surprisingly, with a combination lock. Gabrielle nudged me: the locked room! Reason spun the dial with eager fingers. Noiselessly, the door swung open to reveal a small, apparently windowless room. Lights were already on. Reason ushered us in. I think what we saw bemused each one of us. Along one wall was ranged a battery of computer screens, in the centre a desk with a screen and six phones. For a moment we stood staring beside a grinning Reason; then Virginia DeWitt exclaimed:

'But daddy . . . what *is* this?'

'What is this?' Reason leered. 'A daughter of mine, and you don't know? This is where daddy plays with figures, my love, beginning with small ones and making them grow.'

'You mean . . . still?'

'Why not? It's my life.'

'Oh daddy, but now it's just a game!' She clutched at his arm. 'I'm sorry, so sorry. And you, my father, reduced to this!'

'You silly monkey!' He shook himself free. 'Well, you can call it a game, if you like. It *is* a game. A stupid game. A game men are playing all around the world. But I'm still playing it with the stakes on the board, and all the figures that come up are real.'

'Are real? Oh daddy!'

'Yes – real. Just ask our policeman friend here. George Gently wasn't taken in by the front I put up. And that's what it was, a front. I'm no more bust than Fort Knox. No, I'm still in the business, little girl, and I could buy DeWitt-Oppenheimer twice before breakfast.'

There was horror in her eyes. 'Daddy, you're raving!'

'Then I'm a raving billionaire. Look at this – look, look. This is where I closed on the Hang Seng.'

He went to the desk and tapped in a code. A ten-figure number unrolled on the screen.

'That's in Hong Kong dollars, of course. Here's the total in sterling.'

The ten figures became nine.

'Now the Nikkei Dow – you can have a lot of fun there! Zurich . . . I don't know why I bother . . . Frankfurt . . . Brussels – Brussels is always good for a laugh . . . then the Dow Jones – you see this? And dear old Footsie, where the game began.'

'But it isn't *real*, daddy!'

'What about this?'

He went to a wall safe and spun the lock, took out a bundle of high-denomination notes and pressed it into her trembling hand.

'There, put that in your bag for expenses. And treat Bertie's Hotel as though your father owned it. Because it so happens that he does.'

Poor Virginia DeWitt burst into tears and flopped on the chair at the desk. Reason slapped the safe shut and turned triumphantly to me.

'Fifty million for your house?'

'Oh, Monsieur Charles!' Gabrielle chided. 'If all this is true, why have you behaved so, to make your daughter here so unhappy?'

'Why – why?' His expression changed, the heavy brows lowering.

'The test,' I said.

'Yes, the test. And now the test is complete.'

'You set it up.'

'Who else? I put the rumour round the market. Then I liquidated the lot, every personal asset I possessed. And I've learned what I've learned. I had three daughters, now I've got but one.'

I gestured to the screens. 'And all this is legal?'

His stare was hard. 'Strictly legal. Done through off-shore nominees, computer-programmed. The brain here.'

'And you mean to go on living like this?'

'Since Marie died, what's left?'

'Oh daddy, daddy!' Virginia DeWitt wailed. She'd let the bundle of notes fall to the floor.

But she dried her tears when we returned to the lounge and the truth began to sink in: that her father was not the pauper she had come to rescue, but probably more wealthy than he'd ever been. How wealthy? The computers could have told us, though I doubt if the man himself could. But we did learn that he owned Lime Walk, and was landlord to the owners of those Mercs and Audis. Then, from tears, Virginia DeWitt was bubbling over.

'Daddy, I must go and tell Sue and Olivia!'

At once Reason's face was thunderous. 'That's just what you'll not do, little mouse.' He turned to us. 'And that applies to all present. Not a word to those bitches or anyone else. I want my peace and my security, and I'll have neither if the news gets out. You understand?'

I nodded reluctantly. 'Security I understand.'

'Then take the other for granted. That's something between an old man and his children.'

'But daddy, we must let them know.'

'Not a word I said.'

'But they aren't so terrible, really! I know they haven't behaved very well, but they're still your daughters. And my sisters.'

The wild look was in his eyes. 'You'll make me angry, little girl. They are no longer daughters, no longer sisters. If you love your father you'll say no more.'

'But they may be feeling sorry – '

'I said no more!'

Virginia DeWitt flinched and was silent. Then at once he seemed to regret his rage, drew her to him, kissed the fair hair.

They had planned to lunch at the hotel, and soon afterwards we left them. They passed our window a little later, the father with the daughter on his arm. A strange pair: the untidy old man and the stylish young woman in saxe-blue two-piece; he talking, and bending towards her like a lover, she, solemn-faced, straight-backed, decorous. Yes . . . a strange pair. We watched till they turned the corner of the street. Gabrielle said:

'And I am believing this, that Monsieur Charles is truly still a rich man?'

'I think we must believe it.'

'Aha, you say. But I am thinking perhaps his daughter was nearer to the mark.'

'That he's imagining it all.'

'But yes. Because what are figures on a computer?'

'Don't forget those bank notes.'

'So. His last hundreds. Produced with a flourish to make her believe him.'

I smiled, shaking my head. 'There were other bundles in that safe. Though the whole thing is completely preposterous, on balance I'm having to believe it's true.'

'So then . . . shall we take fifty millions for Heatherings?'

'Not fifty times fifty millions.'

'Then, my friend, let us seek our own lunch, and speak no more of such foolish matters.'

But Gabrielle couldn't quite dismiss such a fascinating business from her mind. She spent the afternoon reading a magazine in the bay window, glancing up alertly whenever, as often happened, someone passed on the pavement. But Reason didn't return after lunch, and neither did his daughter. She, one would have supposed, had retired for a nap, while he, presumably, was pursuing his affairs. For myself, I was minding the phone and fielding such matters as were coming my way; and I was just passing instructions to my colleague, Dutt, when Gabrielle called me to the window.

'See – the lady by the cream car. Just this minute she has parked at his flat.'

The car was a BMW 320, E registration, and the lady had long, flaming chestnut hair.

'Another daughter, yes?'

33

She fitted Capel's description: tall, long-limbed, with dangling ear-rings; and just now an exasperated expression on her face. She was ringing Reason's bell with vigour.

'I think she'll be the eldest, Olivia Welles.'

'So. But I can tell her – she will not find her father in.'

'Look further up the Walk.'

'Aha – that gentleman is not one of ours.'

About fifty yards higher up was parked a metallic red Porsche 924, with leaning on it a hefty young man sporting a mop of fluffy blond hair. Clad in sloppy sugar-bag casual wear, he was watching the lady with absorbed interest.

'You think he comes with her?'

'I suspect a connection.'

'A bodyguard, ha? For the jewels and the furs?'

I shrugged. Small doubt that the silver-mink short coat was as genuine as the adornments of her ears, hands, breast. But now her bold features were narrow with anger as she glared at that unresponding door. She rattled the handle fiercely, then began beating on the door with her fists.

'My faith, she will do herself an injury! I had best go and explain to her, yes?'

'We'll both go.'

Together, we sallied forth from the flat. Becoming aware of us, the lady ceased her attack on Reason's door. Her stare was quelling. She had blazing brown eyes, made the more emphatic with paint, and a wide, painted mouth, at this moment bunched with rage. She stared, then hissed at us:

'Yes?'

'Madame is Monsieur Reason's daughter?' Gabrielle enquired.

'What's that to you, you French bitch?'

34

'Madame! I but come to inform you of where, perhaps, you will find your father.'

'And who are you supposed to be, froggie?'

'Madame, you are not very polite!'

'So sling your hook, froggie. And that goes for your minder, too.'

I grabbed Gabrielle's arm. 'Is it Mrs Welles?'

'Just push off, cheapie.'

'Because if so, your father went to lunch with Mrs DeWitt, who arrived here this morning from New York.'

If I had touched her with a red-hot poker I could scarcely have got a more violent reaction. She gave a sharp, animal-like cry and the brown eyes seemed to explode at me.

'Say that again, you bastard!'

'He went to lunch with Mrs DeWitt.'

'You're lying.'

'It is the truth,' Gabrielle snapped. 'They have gone to Bertie's Hotel, where she is staying.'

'Lies – lies!'

'This morning we are with them. She has come to offer the assistance which some others have denied. To give her love to a grieving old man. Who is not to be deceived by his children, madame.'

I thought she would strike Gabrielle.

'The bitch. The bitch. How can she be here?'

'Rest assured that she is.'

'The lousy little suck-up. And got here this morning?'

Gabrielle merely gave her a withering stare.

'The conniving tramp!' She almost choked. Then her eyes blazed afresh. 'And you precious pair were with him this morning? What games are *you* playing with my father?'

'Madame, you are despicable.'

'Oh yes. Oh yes. And out of what gutter did you come

creeping? I can imagine! You and Miss Innocence. It's a good thing I got here when I did.'

I held Gabrielle very tight! 'We are simple acquaintances, Mrs Welles. By chance we are the present owners of Heatherings, where it pleased your father to come for a weekend.'

'A weekend – you got him for a weekend.'

'He was glad to visit the house again.'

She was breathing hard. 'And that did his business. Your froggie tramp got her little claws into him.'

Gabrielle's claws were close to getting into something, but just then came an interruption. The blond-headed young man had been edging along the pavement and now suddenly, smilingly, he was among us.

'Livvy, you'll make your paint run.' He didn't quite take her arm, but nearly. 'Come on, now! I've been listening. These nice people were only trying to be kind.'

'Get lost, you!'

His smile was invincible. He had blue eyes to go with the hair. Broad-jawed, fair-skinned, an athletic body hidden in the baggy trousers and jacket.

'Didn't they say you'd find him in Bertie's Hotel? Well, then, it's no use hanging on here. Best go and look for him. And I'm sure these good people must realise that you're under a good deal of stress.'

His brilliant smile took in both of us: Mrs Welles's brown eyes stabbed at him.

'You rotten sod. Under stress, am I? Then you'd better watch yourself, for one.'

'Oh, come on, Livvy.'

'Watch out!'

'You know you don't mean half the things you say.'

'Stuff yourself. I do too. And I don't apologise to anyone.'

He gave us a meaning look and a gesture: I decided it was time to take the hint. Olivia Welles bawled something after us as we withdrew, but my hand on Gabrielle's arm was firm. We made the flat. Then she exploded. And Gabrielle can choose her words, even in English.

'Shsh,' I said at last. 'He's got her to leave.'

The BMW came bowling by. Then the Porsche, its blond pilot driving straight-armed; and still smiling.

'Oh, oh,' Gabrielle stormed. 'That *poule* needs a minder if anyone does. I hope they are paying the oaf well, if not he may strangle her himself.'

'I don't think he was her bodyguard.'

'He is not her husband.'

'Say an interested friend.'

'Ha?'

'What do you suppose could have brought her here, in such a state, to visit her father?'

Gabrielle stared with large eyes. 'Oh la! Can Monsieur Charles's secret be out?'

I nodded. 'And that's why she flipped when she learned that his favourite daughter was with him.'

'The test – she has failed it, ha?'

'For her, I think the millions are slipping away.'

'And she is crazy to see him – to change his mind! Oh yes. It is plain now as a shepherd's crook.'

I said: 'I could be wrong. But Mrs Welles has never come this way before. And if that's the case I think we should warn him that his secret is a secret no longer.'

'Oh, my dear. He will be so distressed.'

'Just let me know when you see him return.'

3

When Reason did return, half an hour later, he was clearly
a little the worse for wear; and I watched him fumble
several times before getting his key into the lock. So I
waited another half hour before lifting the phone, and it
was most of a minute later when his blurred voice
answered.

'George Gently. Is it convenient for me to call round
and have a word?'

'Call round . . . any time! Bring your wife too, you
lucky devil.'

I hesitated. 'It could wait.'

'Wait nothing. You come round. Didn't give you a drink
this morning, did I? Something to celebrate, haven't I . . .
what?'

'This could be serious.'

'Nothing's serious. You come round and have a drink.'

So we went round. Reason literally welcomed us with
open arms, giving Gabrielle a kiss on the cheek and
myself a quick hug. Then he hauled us into the lounge,
sat us down, slopped drink into glasses, and insisted on
us toasting the best daughter a man ever had.

'Oh Monsieur Charles!' Gabrielle giggled. 'I fear you
have drunk enough toasts already. You have the bright
eye, monsieur, and a hand that is not so steady. And your
daughter, she is sleeping?'

'Like a bird, my dear, like a little bird in her nest. She rang her husband, gave her daddy a kiss, then tripped off up to bed. Did you ever see such a girl as Ginny?'

'I think monsieur will be spoiling her still.'

'You can't spoil Ginny. She's pure gold. She's poor Marie over again. She shall have the world at her feet, and the world will be the lucky one.'

'Oh monsieur, she is but a woman! Allow her to have a few defects, please. At times she will be late, like other women, and have their foolish fancies, too.'

'Not a word against Ginny!'

'Oh, then, I pity her. For may she not have one little toe of clay?'

'Not one little toe.'

'Then just the nail?'

Reason burst into gusty laughter. 'She is the paragon, my dear, but you don't come so far behind. Your husband is a lucky dog. All men should have such wives. All men.'

'Then all husbands should also be paragons.'

'Drink up. Drink up to Ginny.'

I was reluctant to dispel this mood of euphoria but I felt that Reason had to be told. After a few more toasts to Ginny, I said:

'We met another daughter of yours this afternoon.'

It didn't sink in at once, and when it did he gave his hooded stare.

'What's that?'

'She came in search of you. Mrs Welles, I believe it was.'

'That bitch! In search of me?'

'We advised her she might find you and her sister at Bertie's.'

'But it was me she was after?'

'She was, of course, unaware that Mrs DeWitt was over here.'

The whole craggy structure of his face had changed, the

39

thin-lipped mouth fallen into a droop, the eyes gone small under the gnarled brows, the flushed cheeks shrunken.

'She knows!'

'That was my impression.'

'She knows. She bloody well knows! Nothing else would have fetched the bitch here. Somehow she's got a whiff of the scent.'

'Would that be possible?'

He chewed his lip. 'I thought I'd covered my tracks too well. All done with offshore nominees and a master holding-company in Zurich.'

'But possible to trace it back?'

'Some cunning devil may have got there. They're always trying. And ten to one she'd make it worth their while to split on me.'

'Her husband?'

'Not Freddy. He's in a different line of business.'

'She had a companion, a fair-headed man.'

He shrugged: it didn't strike a note. Then he eyed me. 'So what did you make of her?'

I merely shrugged too.

'Yes,' Reason said. 'Yes. You don't have to spell it out.' His eyes flashed. 'And this you can tell her if ever she shows up here again. She doesn't get a penny, not a brass farthing. And that goes for her bitch of a sister too.'

'But monsieur, is that wise?' Gabrielle exclaimed. 'And I do not say this for any love of that daughter.'

'Not a penny – not a farthing – not the smell of a bank note wrapper! After their treatment of their old father I'll see them walk the streets first.'

'But, better or worse, they are your daughters – and you with so much to give.'

'Nothing. Nothing. They shall have nothing. And don't think this is the whisky talking.' He had a glass in his hand; he hurled it suddenly at the grate, where it smashed into fragments. 'Oh no. This chance was their last. They had too many, and this was the last. I set it up. I couldn't believe that they would turn their backs on their father. But they did. Not a word, not a hand. And so there'll be nothing, nothing, nothing.'

The last three words rose in a crescendo and the old, wild light was in his eyes. For the first time I found myself wondering whether Reason was completely sane. But he took a grip on himself at once: made a gesture of dismissive disgust. Then he reached for the decanter and a fresh glass, and was pouring another drink when the telephone rang.

'Get it for me.'

I got it. The caller was his son-in-law, Frederick Welles. Reason rolled his eyes, then stabbed at a button that enabled us to hear what Frederick Welles had to say.

Reason said: 'Yes, I'm alive, and might even be said to be flourishing.'

A moment of harmonics! Then Welles's apologetic voice:

'Look, Charles, I'm truly sorry that we haven't been in touch. But it wasn't my fault. You sold Belgravia, and I simply didn't have your address.'

'Olivia had it, my man.'

'Yes, I know that now! But she thought it best I shouldn't know. I mean, there were rumours going around.'

'Is that what she's told you?'

'Look, Charles, have a heart. I hold a position of trust. If half those rumours had been true our connection could have been damaging.'

'Damaging to you. Not to Olivia.'

'But it could have rubbed off on me, don't you see? As it was I could feel the draught of being related to a suspected insider. At least, that was the view she took.

41

And all I knew was you'd gone to earth somewhere. I even thought you might have done it deliberately to avoid giving me embarrassment.'

'Would a cheque from your wife have embarrassed you?'

'Charles, I know she's a difficult person. But I've got to stand up for her. She behaved as she did only out of loyalty to me. She just wanted to let the fuss die down. I know, I've been having it out with her. And I know about this afternoon, and that she behaved abominably to some friends of yours.'

'Ah yes,' Reason said. 'Ah yes. She came looking for me this afternoon. And me the same old smelly insider. Wouldn't you say her loyalty slipped a bit there?'

More harmonics!

'Charles . . . let's be frank.'

'Yes,' Reason said. 'Bloody frank.' His eyes glittered. 'You're going to tell me, Freddy, chapter and verse, just how that bitch got past my security.'

'But Charles, I don't know – !'

'Come on, come on.'

'It's the truth. I know only what she's told me. Says one of her friends traced a connection between you and Allgemein Zurich.'

Reason swore. 'What's his name?'

'Honestly, Charles – '

'His name, his name?'

'It's no good, she didn't tell me. Just one of the City set she runs with. I don't know the names of half her friends.'

'It has to be a dealer.'

'I don't know! And I don't know if I should believe it, anyway.'

'But she believes it.'

'Yes.'

Reason swore long and hard. 'So then she comes running to dear daddy, full of the lies she's been telling

42

you, doesn't find me, insults my friends, and puts you up
as her cat's-paw.'

'Charles, I know how it looks – '

'Ha!'

'I admit that Olivia's a difficult person. But she's truly
sorry for this afternoon, and wants me to pass on her
apologies. And then – well!'

'And then what?'

'She tells me that Ginny is in town. I'd like to see both
you and her, and talk things over person to person.'

'You mean I've stopped being a leper?'

'Charles, I'm sorry. I can only say that.'

A little dumb-show! Reason rolls his eyes, Gabrielle
gestures him to give his consent; finally Reason humps
his shoulders, takes a studious pull from his glass.

'Right. But one thing, Freddy. If you come, you come
alone. You can bring all her excuses and apologies, but
Mrs Livvy I will not see.'

We could hear Welles sigh. 'We thought you'd say that.
But she decided she'd better not come, anyway. Later
perhaps.'

'Say never. And if she can't hear me, pass it on.'

Followed an appointment for six-thirty in the lounge of
Bertie's Hotel, and another profession of apologies from
his son-in-law which Reason interrupted by hanging up.
He stared at us with bleak eyes.

'Bloody money. What it buys you.'

'Oh come now, Monsieur Charles,' Gabrielle said. 'Your
Freddy sounded a nice man. And though I cannot say as
much of his wife, even she, it appears, knows when she
behaves badly.'

'So money can buy even that.'

'Then that is one up to money. But in every family these
upsets, ha? And all may yet come right in the end.'

He shook his head. And there was no returning to the

joyous mood in which we'd found him. Somewhere near seventy, he looked older, tireder; saw us out with an absent air.

But then we forgot Reason for a spell.

At the flat, we found friends waiting; John and Brenda Fazakerly, they were fresh back from a jaunt in France. Fazakerly is a photographer, and we couldn't escape it: he'd got his gear under his arm; for the next couple of hours we were seeing slides of the Alps, the Loire and the Côte Fleurie. The latter at least had our attention, since it was in Honfleur that we had first met. We would sooner he had spent longer around the Old Basin, the Place St Catherine, the Côte de Grace. And of course they were curious about that first meeting, a story we didn't want to tell, a story that led to a macabre event which even now Gabrielle shrinks from recalling. So we parried their curiosity, and the talk drifted back to their late trip, to the knitting lady in the toilet at Cabourg, the starlet holding court on *les planches* at Trouville. Then the phone went, and I groaned.

'Sometimes I wish they'd forget my number!'

But it wasn't the Yard. On the phone I was hearing a hysterical, incoherent Reason. And what it seemed he was trying to tell me was that his youngest daughter was dead.

'All right – we'll come straight over.'

There was no getting any sense out of Reason. I went back to the lounge.

'Sorry and all that, but we shall have to shoot you out.'

'Trouble at t'mill?' Fazakerly grinned.

'One of our neighbours with a problem.'

'They sound like ours,' he grinned; but wasted no time

44

in dismantling his gear. When they had gone, Gabrielle grabbed my arm.

'Is it Monsieur Charles?'

'Yes.'

I told her what I'd heard, and her eyes grew very large.

'Can you have heard true?'

'I'm afraid so.'

'Then let us get over there at once, my friend. And let us pray you are mistaken, since if it is true he will be quite crazed.'

Bertie's Hotel isn't far, just down the road in Kensington Church street. A tall, Victorian building, it occupies a site on a corner, and as soon as we had it in view I knew that we could expect the worst. Three squad cars were parked outside it, while a van was just pulling in.

'Alas, poor Monsieur Charles!'

A uniform man on the door stopped us briefly. Then we were through into reception, where the first person I saw was the local CID chief, Detective Chief Inspector Tanner. I grabbed him.

'What's going on?'

'Oh, hullo, sir!' Tanner is an acquaintance. 'We've got a stiff in one of the bedrooms. Looks like a tea-leaf job gone wrong.'

'A girl?'

'Do you know something, sir?'

'Would the victim's name be DeWitt?'

'That's right, sir. Dual nationality. Married to a fellow in New York.'

'Oh, oh!' Gabrielle wailed. Tanner cocked an eye at her.

I said: 'We met her briefly. Her father, Charles Reason, is a neighbour of ours. He rang us, which is why we are here. He sounded in a very disturbed state.'

'You can say that again, sir. He's blown his mind. I've got a WPC smoothing him down.'

'Where is he?'

45

'Through there. Him and a son-in-law who was with him.'

We hastened through to the small lounge where the regulars at Bertie's tend to congregate. Now there was a man on the door and the occupants numbered only three.

'Monsieur Charles – oh Monsieur Charles!'

He sat crouched in a chair, his rheumy eyes staring. Beside him a sturdy-figured WPC. Further off, a sallow-faced man with curly black hair.

'Monsieur . . . monsieur!'

Gabrielle ran to him, dropped on her knee, took his hand in hers. He didn't seem to notice; then, when he did, he pulled his hand away.

'It's no good, miss,' the WPC said. 'You can't get through to him just now. Shock does that to them. But the doctor will give him something when he's through upstairs.'

'Monsieur, it is us – monsieur, monsieur!'

Something clicked in the depths of his eyes. They focused on the kneeling Gabrielle, then jerked away wildly and found me.

'George.'

He struggled out of the chair, almost sending Gabrielle flying. His haggard face was working, his eyes squeezing into a squint. He seized hold of me.

'George.'

'Charlès. I'm very, very sorry.'

'George, get the bastards. Get the swine. Get the devils who did this to Ginny.'

'We'll get them, Charles.'

'Get them. I don't care what it costs. A million. Ten. A hundred. I'll buy the police force. I'll buy London!'

'Hush, hush!'

He was beginning to rave. 'I want those bastards. I want them dead. I'll buy the mafia. I'll put out contracts. I'll – I'll have killers in every street . . . !'

'Just calm down, Charles.'

'I want them dead!'

'Hush, now. We're going to get them.'

'I'll break everyone, I'll smash the banks, I'll buy a bomb and smash the world . . . !'

'Calm down, calm down.'

'Oh Ginny, Ginny. I saw her going up the stairs. She was alive. I saw her go. Oh Ginny, Ginny, Ginny!'

He was clinging to me, howling.

'Shall I fetch Doctor Latham?' the WPC said.

'Just look after him.'

'He needs a sedative.'

I helped the blubbering Reason back to his chair.

'This is terrible,' Gabrielle said. 'I cannot bear he shall be so unhappy. What can we do?'

'You stay with him. I'll send the doctor if he's finished.'

I went back to reception. Tanner was waiting. He gave me a wry look.

'The poor old beggar. Some of them really take it on the chin.'

'Will the doctor be through?'

'I'm going up now, sir. And I've just heard an ambulance is on its way.'

'Who found her?'

'The son-in-law, sir. When she didn't come down he went looking for her.'

'Mind if I come with you?'

'You know better, sir! A bit of luck for me, you strolling in.'

I followed the tall, lanky Tanner up Bertie's sweeping stairs, aware of an audience below penned in the lounge-bar. But upstairs had been cleared, an empty landing, empty corridor: just a DC lounging outside the door of bedroom ten. The door was open. We went in. Ten was one of the expensive rooms, spacious, period drop-ceiling, deep-pile carpet, big sash. Two scene-of-crime officers

were there and a bald-headed man, scribbling notes. And
on a bed Virginia DeWitt. With a towel beneath her bloody
head. I went to look. Her eyes weren't quite closed and
still were not glazed. I touched her hand. Still limp. She
couldn't have been dead for more than an hour.

'Dr Latham?'

'That's me.'

'COD?'

'Blunt instrument.'

'ETD?'

He glanced at his watch. 'Between half-five and half-
six.'

'If you're through you're needed downstairs.'

He nodded. 'I always carry some with me.'

The room had been gone over. Drawers were pulled
out and dumped. The wardrobe door yawned, clothes
were scattered on the floor. The bathroom didn't seem to
have been entered. The chalk outline of the body was
near the outer door. On each door-knob, smeared blood.
If she'd been wearing the crescent brooch, it was gone.
And I saw no sign of the lizard-skin handbag.

'Looks like she caught him at it, sir.'

Yes: that was what it looked like.

'Where are the backstairs?'

'Straight down to the car-park. Not much doubt that's
the way he came. We've had a dose of this sort of caper
lately, but this is the first time we've had a stiff.'

'Any susses?'

'I'll be pulling in a couple. But – ' he nodded to the
door-knobs – 'dabs there won't be.'

I said: 'When I saw her this morning she was wearing
an emerald and diamond crescent brooch. At a guess it
was worth fifty grand, won't be an easy item to fence.'

Tanner shaped his lips in a whistle.

'Then she had a lizard-skin handbag. I saw placed in it

a bundle of fifty-pound notes which would probably add up to another five grand.'

Tanner's face was comical. 'So he really hit the jackpot!'

'When was the call timed?'

'Around six-forty-five, sir, and we were out here before seven. The old boy was in a state like you've seen him, and it was the son-in-law who filled us in. They'd met in the lounge at six-thirty, and the daughter was supposed to join them there. They rang her room, and when she didn't answer the son-in-law went up and found her. Then he rang us.'

'Did he find this door open?'

'Haven't got round to asking him, sir.'

'And the key?'

'The key . . . ?' Tanner stared at it: it was sitting in the lock inside the door, from where it must certainly have been ejected if the lock had been picked. 'Did any of you blokes put that key back?'

The DCs shook their heads, also staring.

'Who was first here.'

'We were, sir. And I'll swear the key was in the lock then.'

Tanner pondered. 'I can't see the son-in-law stopping to put back any keys! I reckon she must have left it unlocked, perhaps nipped out somewhere for a moment. What do you think, sir?'

'It's possible. In that case someone may have seen her.'

'Perhaps she'd already gone down to the lounge, sir, then remembered that she hadn't locked up.'

Then the ambulance men arrived and began unstrapping their stretcher. The body they hoisted on it was quite limp and they had to tuck in the trailing arms. She was dressed in a lime-green evening dress with a split skirt and sheer stockings and silver high-heeled shoes decorated with rhinestones, one of which fell off and had to be placed on the stretcher beside her. They drew a blanket over and made it secure; and humped her away down the backstairs.

'The poor bloody bitch,' Tanner said. The two DCs watched all, said nothing.

We went down again to the regulars' lounge. Doctor Latham was just leaving.

'I've given him a shot . . . if he's still troublesome, I've left some pills with your wife.'

Reason sat groaning, Gabrielle beside him, the WPC standing near and looking bored. The pale-faced son-in-law was also sitting, head resting on his hands. Tanner said to him:

'We'll need your statement, sir. We'll have to ask you to come to the station.'

'You mean – now?'

'If you would, sir. I know you've been through a bit of an ordeal.'

Grey eyes in a pale, oval face, black curls that glinted with brilliantine. Around forty, five-eleven, hairy blunt-fingered hands with a large signet ring. The grey eyes scared.

'But what else can I tell you! I went up there and found her. She was . . . warm. It had only just happened. I must have nearly blundered into him.'

'Did you meet anyone, hear anything, sir?'

'No, or I would have said. I gave her a ring, the desk will tell you. I thought perhaps she was still sleeping off her trip. So I went along to wake her, only to find . . . what I found.'

'Was the door unlocked, sir?'

'The door . . . no! I think I must have found it ajar. That was why I went straight in, after her not answering the ring.'

'What time did you arrive here, sir?'

'Oh, God knows. Some time before half-six.'

'By taxi?'

50

'No, I drove here. My car's outside in the park.'

'Ah.' Tanner's eyes were keen. 'Then you came in by the back way, sir. Would you have noticed anyone hanging about the car-park, or in the entry, on the backstairs?'

'No . . . I don't remember!'

'You might have caught a glimpse of chummie, sir.'

'Well, I didn't. As far as I remember the park and the back way were deserted.'

'And you can't remember the time, sir?'

'Look, I left Eversley Square soon after six. I had to drive here through traffic, probably arrived about twenty-past. I went through to the bar and got a drink. Charles, that's my father-in-law, arrived five minutes later. We gave Ginny ten minutes or so and then I went to the desk and rang her room.'

'So you were the first to arrive, sir.'

'Yes. Yes. The first to arrive.'

'Then, like that, sir – ' Tanner was interrupted by a freezing howl from Reason.

'Blood! I can see blood!'

'Sir, if you'll just keep calm, sir – !'

'Blood. Blood. I can see blood!'

He was on his feet, pointing to his son-in-law's sleeve.

'Blood. Blood!'

And blood there was, a smear on the inside of a cuff. Welles sat petrified, staring at it, his arm turned to reveal it the better.

'But I can explain this! When I found her – '

'Blood. Blood. He killed Ginny.'

'But that's ridiculous, Charles! I got it when I found her, when I lifted her head.'

'Blood. He killed Ginny. He was here when I arrived. And he knew that Ginny would get the money. And the blood's on him. He killed Ginny!'

'Charles, how can you say that – '

'He set it up. He killed her.'

51

'Charles, she was killed by a hotel thief!'

'He set it up. He killed Ginny!'

'Oh Lord, I can't stand this!' Welles covered his face with his hands. 'I liked Ginny, she liked me, I'd never have raised a finger against her. And now she's dead, and Charles – ! He can't believe what he's saying.'

'Easy, easy, sir!' Tanner said. 'We all get upset when these things happen.'

'He killed her,' Reason raved. 'He killed my Ginny.'

'Just you sit down again, sir, and take it easy.'

A plainclothes man came in and took Tanner aside, whispered in his ear. I saw Tanner's face go suddenly alert. He turned to us. Turned to Frederick Welles.

'You did say your car was on the car-park, sir?'

Welles stared blankly. 'That's right.'

'Would it be a blue Rover 800, sir?'

'Yes, but what – ?'

'If I could have the keys, sir?'

'If it's misparked – '

'Just the keys, sir. And I'd like you to stay here.'

After a pause Welles produced the keys, threw them pettishly on the floor.

'Thank you, sir.' Tanner picked them up, nodded to his man, nodded to me. The man stayed put by the door, I followed Tanner out of the lounge. I said:

'What was all that about?'

'You'll soon see, sir. And if it's true, we've got our man.'

'You mean – Welles?'

'You'll see. Didn't you tell me she had a lizard-skin handbag?'

We hustled through the back corridor, past the stairs down which the stretcher had come, out to the small car-park, dimly lit by nearby street-lights. There, another of Tanner's men was waiting by a midnight-blue Rover 800.

'Shine your torch.'

He shone it first on the door-handle on the driver's side. No question: both handle and adjacent paintwork were smeared with blood.

'Now inside.'

Through the tinted glass it wasn't so easy to get a view, but plainly sticking out from beneath the driver's seat was the corner of a lizard-skin handbag.

'Right . . .'

Tanner used the key on the passenger side, leaned across to unlock and push open the driver's door. Then we saw everything. The bag. The crescent brooch, shoved under with it. A pair of blood-soaked woollen gloves. The handle of a jack, protruding bloodily. We stared long, but touched nothing. Then Tanner relocked the car.

'Oh dear, sir! And me almost believing in that tea-leaf.'

'Is there blood on those keys?'

The torch was shone on them, but no blood was apparent.

'Could have rubbed off in his pocket. But we've got all the blood we need. You satisfied, sir?'

I shrugged; they'd got enough to do Welles twice over. And motive enough for ten. Even though only figures on a computer.

4

We took him out and showed him. He was silent as we marched him to the car. Then, when he saw that damning evidence, his sallow face went white.

'But that . . . that's impossible!'

'Can you explain it, sir?'

'Someone – !' His livid lips clamped tight. His face was ghastly in the glimmer from the street-lights and he rocked slightly, seemed near a faint.

'Did you put these things here, sir?'

He couldn't speak, just shook his head.

'So I'm afraid I'm going to have to arrest you, sir, on suspicion of having murdered your sister-in-law.'

He made a whining sound, but his lips stayed clamped. We marched him back into the hotel. He was tottering, dragging his legs, was helped along by one of the DCs. Then, in reception, under a hundred eyes, he gabbled:

'I want to make a phone-call!'

'You can do that later at the police station, sir.'

'No. I want to ring my wife.'

Tanner glanced at me; I grimaced. Sooner or later she would have to be told. We shored him up at the desk in reception and pulled the phone towards him. He could barely hold it, tap in the number. The ring was answered almost at once.

'Olivia . . . Ginny's dead! Someone killed her . . .

they're arresting me. Olivia – do something, Olivia! Get our solicitor . . . do something, please!'

At the other end, a chirping voice; at this, Welles's eyes in desperate despair.

'Olivia, you can't mean that . . . Olivia, Olivia! No, Olivia. No . . . please!'

But the line went dead on him, and the phone slipped from his fingers.

Tanner said kindly: 'We'll let you ring again, sir. You can ring your solicitor from the station.'

He didn't seem to hear. And the door of the small lounge had suddenly swung back to reveal Reason.

'Let's get him away!'

We hustled him out, across the pavement, into a squad car. Behind us Reason was howling threats, with the WPC hanging on to his arm; and the patrons in the lounge-bar, no longer to be restrained, came pouring out to see the fun. Gabrielle broke through them and ran to me.

'My dear, he's quite crazy. What can we do?'

'Stay with him. I must go to the station. Try to get him back to the flat.'

'This I will do. But oh, it is terrible. How can things like this happen?'

I pressed her hand, jumped in after the prisoner, and we were away with siren blaring. I could feel Welles beside me shaking violently, hear his low keening, like that of a trapped animal. The police station was but a few streets away. It seemed a temple of peace after the furore at Bertie's. We helped Welles in, booked him, sat him down in an interview-room with a uniform-man; then Tanner ordered coffee to be fetched and led me off to his office.

'For crying out – we do see life, sir! I expect the press will go to town on this one.'

'They will if Reason's secret leaks out.'

'Yes, sir. I was going to ask you about that.'

55

Lean, gawky, cockney, his whimsical face alight with curiosity, Tanner placed a chair for me, then threw himself down behind his desk. I let it drift till the coffee came and I'd lit my pipe. Then I told him.

'You mean . . . he was never bust at all?'

'No. To the best of my knowledge he's a millionaire in three continents.'

'Like he's one of those eccentric bleeders one hears about?'

'I'm afraid there's more to it than that. He sold up and put the rumours about deliberately to see how his family would respond. A test he called it. To let them think he was broke and perhaps guilty of shady practices.'

Tanner's face wrinkled. 'The soft old sod! Always begging your pardon, sir.'

'To be kind, he was disturbed at the time by the death of a very dear wife.'

Tanner shook his head. 'And all that money. I reckon that would drive anyone off the rails. Not that I'd pass up the risk myself, sir. But there has to be a limit. Even with money.'

'Beyond the first million,' I said.

'Perhaps the first two, sir. To be on the safe side.' Tanner whiffed at the cheroot he'd put on. 'And what happened tonight is all along of that?'

'All along of that. Two children failed the test. The youngest daughter, his favourite, didn't. She flew in this morning from New York with the offer of a directorship in her husband's firm. Then he let her know. We were there. And no doubt where he was going to leave his millions.'

Tanner screwed up his face. 'Suppose she couldn't have found out, sir?'

I took a puff. 'Highly unlikely.'

'I mean . . . the others seem to have got on to it?'

I shook my head. 'I was there. Forget it.'

56

'If you say so, sir. But the others did get on to it.'

'The eldest daughter has acquaintances in the City. According to Reason a curious dealer could have traced beneficial ownership back to him.'

'The eldest being chummie's wife.'

'Right. And she knew by the latest this afternoon. She arrived in Lime Walk in a disturbed state, seeking an interview with her father. He was at Bertie's Hotel with Mrs DeWitt, but if she looked for him there she didn't find him. I thought it best he should be told, and it was while we were with him that Welles rang up and arranged to meet them.'

'He set it up, sir.'

'Reason switched the phone so we could hear him.'

'No question that he knew about the old man's money?'

'None. He admitted hearing it from his wife.'

Tanner puffed shrewdly. 'So it all fits together. He set it up, then he carried it out. He gets there ahead of the old man, sneaks up the backstairs, knocks on her door. Which is why we found the key still in the lock.'

'She opened to him.'

'So then he does his little job, roughs the room up, sneaks back to his car with the loot and the gubbins, and he's sitting in the lounge with a drink when the old man turns up at six-thirty.'

'We shall need to know when he left his house.'

'Yes, sir, I'll get on to it.'

'And a trace of blood on the car-keys would help.'

'Ten to one he left the car unlocked.'

We kicked it around some more, then Latham's bald head appeared round the door. He said:

'I've checked him over. But if you were hoping for blood on his hands I must disappoint you.'

I said: 'He'd have been wearing woollen gloves, and they had the appearance of being well-soaked.'

He shook his head. 'It couldn't have got through. But I've taken swabs and I'll let you know.'

'Any other visible blood?'

'None. Just the smear on the cuff.'

He went. Tanner hoisted lean shoulders. 'It would almost have been too much, sir!'

'In homicide, nothing is too much.'

'All the same, sir . . . along with the rest.' He puffed, stubbed the cheroot, rose and stretched his lanky frame. 'Shall we go and hear what chummie has to talk about?'

I knocked out my pipe and we went.

Welles had been stripped and his clothes sent to forensic and now he sat huddled in a couple of blankets. He didn't look up as we entered the interview-room, kept staring at the lino-topped table and its sheaf of statement-paper. Tanner dismissed the constable, took the chair opposite, across the table. I pulled one up at the end. Tanner leaned elbows, stared at the prisoner.

'Would you like to smoke, Welles?'

Welles stayed silent, pulled the blankets closer.

Tanner said: 'We can do this the easy way, you just telling us what happened. Save us trouble, save you trouble. If you like, you can write it down.'

Welles stared at him. Tanner sighed.

'You're in the cart, Welles, and you know it. But we're not the Gestapo, we can be your friends. All we're asking is co-operation.'

Welles's lip quivered. 'You won't believe me.'

'Try us,' Tanner said. 'Try us.'

'I didn't kill her. I didn't.'

Tanner looked at him long and hard. 'So who did?'

'It had to be a thief.'

'A thief,' Tanner said, 'who owns your car.'

58

'No, but listen! I've been sitting here thinking. It's the only way it could have happened.'

'Go on,' Tanner said. 'Go on.'

'He was going to steal my car too. Then something, someone scared him and he simply ran off.'

'Without the loot,' Tanner said. 'Five thousand nicker and a brooch worth Christ knows how much?'

'Yes. Something scared him.'

'Must have,' Tanner said. 'Like he couldn't help locking your car before he left.'

'That could have been accidental!'

Very slowly, Tanner's head began to shake. 'Nice try,' he said. 'Nice try. I hear a lot of these, and this is a good one. You got any more you'd like to tell me?'

'But if I didn't do it . . .'

'Keep going,' Tanner said.

'Oh God, that has to be the answer.'

'If you didn't do it.'

'But I didn't!'

'Where we came in,' Tanner said. He sighed yet more deeply. 'You see how it is,' he said. 'Me, I don't mind you telling me a tale, all part of life's rich tapestry. But it holds up the action, makes grief. Because you're in the shit, you know it, we know it. So just co-operate, that's the deal. Then we can sort it out like friends.'

'But you don't believe me!'

'Like friends,' Tanner said. 'Just tell us what happened.'

Welles stared at him with baffled eyes. Then his teeth clicked and his mouth shut tight. He dragged the blankets even closer, returned his stare to the lino top.

'The money,' Tanner said. 'You knew about the money.'

He didn't want to answer, but it was dragged out of him.

'I only knew what Livvy told me. It could have been true, or just another rumour.'

'Livvy being your wife?'

'Yes! One of her friends . . . I don't know. She was believing it, anyway. That Charles wasn't bust and never had been. That he was behind one of the big internationals.'

'Allgemein Zurich,' I said.

He flung me a look. 'You seem to know.'

'And what would that make him?'

'If it were true, a billionaire several times over.'

'But you didn't know if it were true?'

The same baffled look. 'It could have been true or false. After all the other rumours about Charles, this one seemed a bit much to swallow.'

'Did he deny it himself?'

'I – not exactly! Look, I can't tell how much you know. But the fact is I couldn't be certain. I don't know whether to believe it now.'

I said: 'When did you first hear the rumour?'

'Just this afternoon, when I got home. I found Livvy in one of her stews, she'd only recently heard it too. She'd gone looking for her father but hadn't found him. And she'd heard that Ginny was over on a visit. Well, she'd put two and two together and convinced herself that Ginny was after the money.'

'And that was also your opinion?'

'No. I doubt if Ginny could have cared less. I mean, her husband was a millionaire already, and anyway Ginny wasn't that sort.'

'Yet whether or no, it would have been left to her?'

His eyes darted about, as though seeking an escape.

'All right then – if you want a straight answer! Yes and yes. It would have gone all to her.'

'You knew that?'

'Yes. I knew it.'

'Because of the way your wife had behaved?'

'All right, all right. Because of that.'

'When she thought her father was flat broke.'

His hands gripped the blankets, but his hands were shaking. 'That isn't fair either, what you're saying! Being Charles's daughter isn't all honey – he can be a tyrant, you understand? And if she's got a temper, then she got it from him – oh no! You can't blame it all on Livvy.'

'This afternoon, her mood was scarcely conciliatory.'

'This afternoon . . . oh Lord! Was it you?' A glaze seemed to go over the grey eyes. 'Then I know what to expect, don't I? But I'll say it just the same. She isn't so bad. When she had cooled down she knew she'd behaved foolishly. She was sorry. She wanted to say sorry – to you, to her father, to poor Ginny. And it was because of her, no one else, that I arranged to meet them this evening.'

'The suggestion came from her . . . ?'

'Yes, from her, even though it doesn't suit your book. Oh, I admit I would have gone anyway to try to smooth things over. But it was Livvy who was urging me to it. She genuinely wanted to make up. And she knew it was no use going herself, because it would only have landed her in a flaming row.'

Tanner was giving him a sideways look. 'You're saying it wasn't you who set this up?'

'No – yes! It was me who arranged it. But only to make up with Charles and Ginny.'

'Just to make up. Then you had a rush of blood.'

'Oh God, no. Why can't you believe me?'

'All that money,' Tanner said. 'Plenty for everyone. Only it had wings. Someone had to clip them.'

Welles just groaned and hugged the blankets.

'We can understand it,' Tanner said. 'You could have gone up there just to talk to her, see if you couldn't work out a deal. Only maybe you had an inkling that wouldn't wash, and somehow the jack-handle went along with you. As you were driving there. A rush of blood. Settle the business once and for all. Wasn't it like that?'

Welles keened through his teeth.

'Then it had to look good,' Tanner said. 'A robbery, muss up the room, grab some loot and stash it away. You hadn't much time, it had to go in your car, but who the hell would search that? So away with it quick, then through to the bar to settle your nerves with a stiff drink.' Tanner did his sighing act. 'Why can't we be friends about this?' he said. 'You're not the first, won't be the last. And you're never going to walk away from it.'

'But I – didn't – do it.'

'Oh, come on now. Let's forget and start again.'

Welles keened, hugged, rocked a little in his blankets.

I said: 'Let's nail this down. What time do you say you left your house?'

'I don't know . . . after six. I live in Eversley Square, that's Belgravia.'

'Who can vouch for that?'

'Livvy.'

'Apart from your wife?'

He shook his head. 'We have a housekeeper living-in. But she's away most weekends.'

'And when you arrived at Bertie's Hotel?'

'It couldn't have been much before six-thirty.'

'Did anyone at all see you park?'

He shook his head, went on shaking it.

'And when you came through from the car-park?'

'No. No. Until I got to the bar.'

I looked at Tanner.

'Hard on half-past, sir. And the barman noticed he was looking upset.'

'Upset?'

'Oh my God!' Welles burst out. 'Yes, I was upset, wouldn't you have been? I was there to make my peace

62

with Charles, and I knew I could expect no mercy from him.'

'So only your wife can say when you left home, and nobody can vouch for when you parked at Bertie's?'

'All right, yes. I haven't a leg. If you've got to have someone, it had better be me.'

'Is that a confession?'

He gritted his teeth. 'I didn't, didn't do it. I don't care. You can ask till doomsday. I didn't do it. I didn't.'

'Someone did it.'

'Not me.'

'Someone who locked the weapon in your car.'

'Not me. The thief.'

I stared at him. 'You'd better not tell that tale in court.'

He keened and keened. He wasn't ill-looking. The sweating face had some good features. I could imagine him arming the dashing creature who had thrown insults at us that afternoon: at a happier time. I said:

'If you think you can raise your solicitor you can make that call.'

'I don't want to.'

'I think you'd be advised.'

His eyes were wretched. 'Does that mean . . . ?'

I stared. Still his eyes clung.

'Livvy . . . she didn't want to know.'

'I expect she found the news a shock.'

'But if she abandons me, too . . .'

A knock at the door interrupted and a uniform sergeant entered. He stared at the prisoner, then at us, and made a motion with his head. We followed him out. He said:

'There's a bit of a scene going on out front, sir. The dead girl's father is there, and now chummie's wife. She came back in the car we sent to fetch him some clothes.'

'Oh lor'!' Tanner said. 'That's all we need. Well, we weren't getting very far with chummie. See he gets his

63

clobber, will you. Perhaps it won't hurt him to stew for a while.'

He gave me a grimace. We went through to reception. And the sergeant was right: there was a scene going on.

It was truly dramatic: Reason was planted there, a towering, glowering figure of rage: and, at his feet, the kneeling, imploring form of Olivia Welles. Gabrielle was there, but merely as chorus, and the audience was a couple of uniform men. Olivia Welles was clasping her father's knees and giving vent to decorous sobbings. It lasted just seconds: then Reason caught sight of us and kicked his wailing daughter away.

'Has the devil confessed? Has he? I want a confession. I will have one!'

'Oh father, you're cruel!' Olivia Welles sobbed. 'How can you believe that poor Frederick is guilty?'

'Quiet, you hypocritical bitch! Has he confessed – have you wrung it out of him?'

I said: 'The enquiry is proceeding. But you must leave it in the hands of the police.'

'The police – the police. I want a confession!'

'We are doing everything we can.'

'But it's not enough, do you hear? Not if the devil hasn't confessed.'

'You must leave it with us.'

'Use racks. Use thumbscrews. Hang him up by his heels till he spits. I'll buy justice. I'll buy your indemnity. Only let me hear the monster confess.'

'Oh father, father!'

'A monster I say! Out of his own mouth I must hear it.'

'Father, you're mad.'

'Aha, he'll find so. Must I wrest it from him with these two hands?'

'Monsieur Charles,' Gabrielle pleaded. 'It won't do, monsieur. Your loss is cruel, but there must be patience.'

'Patience – with her blood still wet on his sleeve?'

'Yes, monsieur, patience. Or you will run mad.'

I saw Olivia Welles slide her a look.

'I'll be patient,' Reason stormed. 'Let me hear him say it, then I'll be patient, if I can. Until then patience is a noise, the empty air, nothing. Yes, I'm mad, and mad I'll stay. Patience has gone out of fashion.'

'All this helps nothing, monsieur.'

'Who helped my daughter? Who helped Ginny?'

'It is cruel, but you must abide it.'

'Must I? Must I? Oh, Ginny, Ginny!'

'Father, poor father!'

Olivia Welles sought to embrace Reason again. Once more he thrust her from him, but she was not to be denied.

'You still have us, father. You still have Susan and me. We love you. We'll make it up to you. We'll help you forget this terrible thing.'

'Stay out of my path, you she-wolf.'

'Oh father, you're so unfair! I stayed away because I thought you were angry with me, not because I didn't care.'

'Tell your lies to your husband.'

'How can you say that? When all I want is to care and help? You're so wrong about me, father, so wrong! I'm your daughter too, don't push me away from you.'

But he did. Then he grabbed me. 'Have you charged that devil yet?'

'Our investigation is not complete.'

'Then he hasn't confessed. No confession!'

'Your son-in-law denies knowledge of the deed.'

'But he did it. And you know he did it.'

'We only know that the evidence is very strong. But the

investigation is continuing. It may be that a charge is the most likely result.'

The staring eyes had their crazy look and the grip on my arm was painful. His face came closer.

'But you've got him. No way he's ever going to walk free.'

'As I said, the evidence is very strong.'

'No miserable counsel can get him off?'

'I can only repeat. The evidence is strong.'

'Stop it, stop it!' Olivia Welles cried. 'Father, how can you be so vindictive? It's all a mistake, Freddy couldn't have done it, he only went there to apologise for my being so beastly.'

Father transferred stare to daughter. 'And if I told you what you think you've found out isn't true?'

'Isn't – true?' The brown eyes were staring like two stones from between the chestnut locks.

'If I'm still a poor man?'

Hate blazed in the eyes.

'Money,' Reason snarled. 'That was what your devil husband came after. Money. And if money can buy anything, he'll never see the outside of a prison cell.'

'Oh, you're wicked!' Olivia Welles cried. 'Who cares about your money? I don't want it. I want my husband. You can keep all the rest.'

'The devil shall pay.'

'Oh, wicked, wicked!'

'He killed Ginny. He's going to pay.'

'No, no, he never did.'

'He killed her. He killed Ginny.'

Then his face crumpled, he pulled away, felt for a chair, collapsed on to it. Gabrielle went to him, laid her hand on his shoulder. Olivia Welles watched her with seething eyes. To her I said:

'Just a couple of questions.'

She turned her blazing gaze on me.

66

'What time did your husband leave the house this evening?'

'Why don't you ask him?'

'I'm asking you.'

She went on savaging me with her eyes. 'I didn't know who you were this afternoon, did I? Some little hanger-on, I thought, with a female attachment as cunning as yourself. Well, I haven't changed my mind. You're in the saddle, better make the most of it. But if you think my father's a fool, then you haven't found out yet who you're dealing with.'

'But in answer to the question?'

'How should I know?'

'Were you not in the house at the time?'

Sweeping lashes narrowed imperceptibly over eyes that never winked.

'Do you think I shall help you trap my husband? You must be a bigger fool than I thought. But it doesn't signify, since he didn't do it. So I may as well answer your silly question.'

'Well?'

'Of course I was in the house. Hadn't I just been straightening Freddy out about father? Who I didn't find at Bertie's incidentally, where my dear sister had just gone up to bed.'

'And?'

'Freddy rang father and arranged to meet them both at six-thirty. And in due course he did just that, leaving me to stare at the television.' Her lip curled. 'And what time did he leave – meaning did he have time to bash Ginny? Well, let's see. It wouldn't have taken long. Give it ten minutes in either direction.'

'So.'

'Let me think! As I said, I was watching television. *The Flying Doctors*, I seem to remember. And the programme changes at six.'

'He left before six?'

'Do your own mathematics. If so, only by a little. Whether enough or not you will doubtless know, but it doesn't matter. Because he didn't do it.' Then the look was sidelong. 'Do I get to see Freddy?'

'That won't be possible tonight.'

'So.' A swirl of the hair. 'Better give him my love, then, and provide me with a car back to Eversley Square.'

Turner winked at me and gave the order. Before she left, Olivia Welles turned again to her father. He wouldn't look at her, sat staring ahead, the grey-blue eyes without focus. She said softly:

'You're wrong, you know.'

It didn't provoke a reaction. Perhaps, at long last, the doctor's sedative was taking effect, was easing the turmoil in that shaggy head. Olivia Welles eyed Gabrielle balefully, then stalked out to the car. Tanner slid me a look.

'Whew! Perhaps chummie is safer off inside, sir. Why do you think she picked him?'

I simply shrugged.

'Me, I'd sooner stay poor and happy,' Tanner said.

5

Till now nothing further had come to hand to augment the case against Welles. No member of the hotel staff had seen him park or had a sight of him until he appeared in the bar. A fellow-guest of Mrs DeWitt's had been in his room at the time when the attack must have taken place, but he'd had the television on and had heard nothing untoward. Meanwhile Latham had checked his swabs and come up with a negative result. He had also examined the blood-soaked gloves, about which he could only advance a theory.

'If he discarded the gloves at once, the blood might not have had time to soak through.'

'Not even a trace?'

'It's possible. It depends on how soon he got rid of them.'

'And the car-keys?'

'Negative too.'

We'd have to assume an unlocked car when Welles made his first entry: not unlikely that he'd leave the door touch-shut to avoid the noise of slamming it. But something fresh to hit him with would have helped.

Tanner said: 'Do we have another go at him?'

I shook my head. 'Let him sleep on it.'

Tanner nodded. 'I think that's the drill, sir, give him time to chew it over. But what about the old boy?'

'We'll take him off your hands.'

In fact Reason had stayed quiet since the departure of Olivia Welles. He was still sitting hunched on the chair in reception, his empty eyes staring, staring. I went up to him.

'Charles.'

The eyes slowly lifted, met mine.

'We're leaving, Charles. You too. You'd better come along with us.'

His mouth worked. 'George . . . where is she?'

'Where . . . ?'

'Ginny. Where have they taken her?'

'Oh, do not think of such things!' Gabrielle exclaimed. 'Just come with us, Monsieur Charles.'

'But where . . . where . . . ?'

'It is taken care of. All, everything is taken care of. Tonight, no more, ha? You are with friends. You come with us.'

He looked at her stupidly. 'With you?'

'But yes. Just for this night.'

'I'll get you a car, sir,' Tanner said. 'The old boy looks as though he needs one.'

It came. We helped him into it. Only for a moment did trouble seem likely. On the pavement he shook himself free and turned to stare at the police station with savage eyes. Something he snarled, I couldn't hear what; but it ended in a whimper. Then he was in the car, and we were accelerating away.

But it wasn't to be an easy night, for all the valium Latham had left with us. At the flat we sat him down in the lounge while Gabrielle went to brew coffee and prepare a snack meal. I switched on the TV, very low. It was an orchestra playing Mozart. Reason gazed at the screen for some minutes, but his eyes weren't following the switches of the camera. Finally his head jerked back.

'I could ruin Freddy's bank, you know that? I could take it over, close it down, and never know I'd spent the money.'

I shrugged. 'The bank's not to blame.'

'And the rest, the rest! There's a crash coming. Press a few buttons, and I could start it, throw all these pips-queaks into the gutter.'

'What good would that do?'

'Let them suffer. Let them feel it where it hurts. The means are there. The money's there. Wall Street, Tokyo and London. And why not, why bloody not? When not every penny will bring her back to me.'

'Hush!' Gabrielle said, at the door.

'Not every dollar – every yen! Marie, Ginny, it couldn't save them. I'll press those buttons, smash the world.'

It was the first of a number of such outbursts. Each time they ended in hysterical sobbing. Occasionally he would talk quite rationally for a spell, but always the mood of insane threats returned. At other times he sat staring at nothing, oblivious of whatever was going on around him. Poor Gabrielle was in despair.

'Monsieur, you must not give in in this way. You are a man, yes, one of strong character, and you behave not as you should.'

'And to think that I trusted him!'

'Monsieur!'

'As late as this evening, I trusted Freddy. I could have sworn . . .' His eyes snapped. 'That bitch – that bitch has got at him.'

'Do not speak so!'

'The bitch – arrest her! Strip her, throw her into a dungeon. I'll ruin her, I'll ruin him. I'll bring the world about their ears.'

'This is madness, monsieur!'

71

'When Tokyo opens . . .'

And the sobbing commenced again.

It all ended suddenly, though not till the small hours; his strength could probably take no more. What had been a fit of sobbing became a fit of snoring, and Reason slewed sideways on the settee. Pointless to think of undressing him. We tucked his legs up, put a cushion beneath his head and spread blankets over him. Then we retired, leaving open doors so that we might hear any movement of his during the night.

'My dear, such a day I would not live through again.'

I grunted as I put out the light.

'But what shall happen to this poor man?'

I didn't know, and for the moment didn't care.

In the morning we found him as we had left him, snoring away on the settee, and it was not till breakfast was on the table that we heard the cistern flush in the bathroom. He arrived a few minutes later, looking weary but somewhat more himself, and, after a grumpy 'good-morning', sat down at the place set for him. Gabrielle poured coffee. He ignored it.

'So what happens now?'

I shrugged. 'The inquiry continues.'

'I mean what bloody happens! Do you get a confession, or don't you?'

'We shall try. In light of the evidence a confession is scarcely necessary. I think you may take it as fairly certain that Welles will be charged later today.'

'Money won't help?'

'No.'

'I'm not talking about hundreds and thousands!'

I dunked a croissant, said nothing. Reason glared across the table.

'Look, last night I was knocked out – all I could think

about was poor Ginny . . .' His mouth trembled an instant, but then locked firm again. 'Freddy. He'd never have done it. Not on his own is what I mean! That bitch, that she-wolf put him up to it. And you've got to get her too.'

'We have no evidence . . .'

'Bugger your evidence! Don't I know my own daughter? She was behind it. She went straight home and set the bloody thing going. Freddy, he was just putty. She was standing over him when he phoned. And then mutt went and bungled it – he could have thrown that gear down anywhere . . .'

'I repeat, we have no evidence.'

'Motive – motive is the evidence!'

I sipped coffee. 'Not enough.'

Reason looked as though he would have bitten me.

'Listen. Money. Real money. Not the ha'pence that dazzles yuppies. Money that makes and breaks markets. Money that sets up, knocks down governments. And it's there, behind those computers. And someone let on that it was there. Only Ginny, poor Ginny was in the way . . .' Again his mouth trembled; was screwed tight. 'Livvy had queered her pitch, she knew that, there was only one way to the money. And if it drove me mad, so much the better – she could take over, wouldn't have to wait.'

'Oh Monsieur Charles, she could not be so wicked!' – Gabrielle was gazing with wide eyes.

'Oh yes. Oh yes. To get to the money Livvy would kill. And perhaps kill again.'

'Monsieur, you are still not yourself.'

'I know my daughter. I know her!'

'She is spoiled, she is greedy, yes? But not this evil thing you would make her.'

He turned wild eyes on me. 'But listen. Livvy comes looking for me at the hotel? Not her, not her, her mind is made up, she's casing the joint for the evening.'

73

'Oh, that is too crazy!'

'Freddy knew the number of Ginny's room!'

'Perhaps she is mentioning this, yes, but not for the terrible reason you say.'

He closed his eyes, and through his teeth said: 'A confession. Or nothing is done. She'll stay free. I shall be in her way. And there can be only one end to that.'

I was about to reply when there came a squeak of tyres and a car pulled up outside. A red Golf GTi convertible, it had its roof down. A snub-nosed young lady jumped out.

'I'm Suzy Strickland. My father is here. Please, you must let me in to see him!'

Slim, lithe, about five-seven, with freckles and a plangent voice. In a roll-top sweater and pleated skirt beneath which bare legs.

'You are Charles Reason's daughter?'

'Yes – yes! I've only just got back from abroad. Then I rang Livvy and heard the frightful thing that happened last night. Please, may I come in? Daddy must be absolutely starkers.'

'If you'll kindly wait here – '

'Oh please! Don't worry, I can handle daddy.'

And she pushed past me; but Reason had already emerged into the hall. With a cry, she darted towards him, caught him in an embrace and began covering his unshaved cheeks with kisses.

'Daddy. Oh daddy.'

'Get off, you slut!'

'Oh daddy, I've only just heard! I got back last night, and didn't ring Livvy till this morning.'

'And you've wasted no time.'

'Oh, dear daddy! I know what you're thinking, but it wasn't my fault. Livvy told me you wouldn't see me, and swore she didn't know your address.'

'You lying hussy!'

'It's true, daddy. I've been trying to find out where you were. But Livvy said – because of the divorce – well, you didn't want me darkening your doors . . .'

'And you think I'll swallow that, you monkey?'

'But it's true, it's true, it's true! And now this ghastly thing has happened, and I just want to be with you, to be at your side.'

'Get off me, Jezebel!'

'I'll do anything – '

Reason gave her a shove that sent her staggering. Her eyes flashed at him and she stood pouting and breathing hard through her snubbed nostrils. I said hastily:

'Shall we go through – ?'

After a pause, Susan Strickland plunged through into the lounge. There she threw herself on the settee and burst into loud lamentations.

'He doesn't love me any more! Oh why, why did I listen to Livvy?'

'Shut up!' Reason snarled. 'You're here for one thing. Livvy has told you about the money.'

'I don't care about that. I don't care about anything. You don't love me any more. Livvy has told you a pack of lies.'

'She didn't have to.'

'Then why are you against me? It has to be rotten Livvy's doing.'

'You can blame yourself.'

'No! I've always been a loving daughter.'

Reason glared at us. 'They're in league,' he snapped. 'Livvy has set this bitch on. She knows she can't fool the old man, so she's sent this one to play her games.'

Susan Strickland wailed piteously.

'Monsieur, you are too hard,' Gabrielle chided. 'It is, after all, your daughter, who is showing a wish to be kind.'

75

'For my money – not for me.'

'At least, a chance you should give your child. This terrible trouble perhaps makes you too quick, too soon to suspect bad things, ha?'

Reason stared savagely at his weeping daughter. 'This one turned her back too. From Livvy I expected no less, but I deserved better from Susie-Lu. I forgave her a marriage that grieved poor Marie. I forgave her a scandalous divorce. She made a pretence of loving the old man. But she turned her back as soon as the other.'

'It wasn't my fault – I explained that!'

His eye was piercing. 'I've heard explanations from your sister too. And I'm to swallow them?'

'Oh daddy, Livvy is a liar, you know you can't believe a word she says.' Susan Strickland sat up eagerly. 'But what I told you was the truth. I just didn't know where to find you – did you really think I didn't try? And it's no pretence that I love you – I do, I do! And you need me now.'

Still Reason's stare was unforgiving. 'Miss went looking for me in Cannes?'

'Daddy, please don't use that tone. I was so unhappy, I had to get away. I couldn't find you, and Livvy swore blue you wouldn't see me if I did. I couldn't bear it. I just felt I must go a long way away.'

Reason grunted; but his aspect was softening. 'Well, you and your Maker know the truth of it.'

'I want to love you. I want to help you.'

Reason shook his head with a deep sigh.

The coffee was cold; Gabrielle made a fresh pot, and pressed croissants and jam on father and daughter. But the situation was tinder. They ate, drank in silence, each intent on their own thoughts. Susan Strickland was scowling to herself, Reason had withdrawn into lethargy. I could see Gabrielle priming herself once or twice with a remark, but each time she felt obliged to desist. I hoped the phone would ring. It didn't. Finally, Susan Strickland lit herself a cigarette.

'Daddy, what can we do about Freddy?'

Reason came out of his abstraction with a bang. 'Do? We have to sit on our hands and wait for this gentleman to arrange his future.'

'But – can't we do something?'

Reason snorted. 'Money. No. It's been tried. Money buys murder, not justice.' His lips quivered. 'Bloody murder!'

Susan Strickland looked down her snub nose. 'But daddy, there must be something. I mean witnesses, alibis, that sort of thing. If we looked properly, I'm sure we'd find them.'

'What – what?'

'You know what I mean. People who could place Freddy somewhere else. There's sure to be some. All they need is persuasion to come forward.'

Reason's brows couldn't have hooked higher. 'I – pay – to get him off?'

'I didn't say that! But – well, you know. I'm certain you can do it if anyone can.'

Reason jerked his head violently. 'I'm not hearing this. I didn't hear my daughter speak.'

'Oh, daddy!'

'No. No. It must be true. My brain is going.'

'Daddy, be sensible!'

'Her sister's killer. The devil who took poor Ginny's life. For money, money, money – and I'm to pay bribes to fetch him off?'

Now it was the daughter's brows lifting. 'But daddy, he didn't do it, and you know he didn't!'

'I know? With the blood on his sleeve, and the blood and the jewels in his car?'

77

'No – he didn't!' Her plangent voice was suddenly a note harsher. 'All that was faked – planted by the police – they had to come up with someone, didn't they?'

'Planted!'

'Yes. Planted. Because poor Freddy went up and found her. Because he'd got that blood on his sleeve. Because you invented a motive for him. But he didn't do it, because he couldn't, and no one who knows him would ever dream it. Freddy's gentle, Freddy's lovely, and you've got to get him off.'

For an instant Reason was staggered. Then he snarled: 'Ask Livvy.'

'Livvy?'

'She's behind it. She can tell you who did it.'

Susan Strickland was screaming. 'And you'd believe her – a filthy bitch like precious Livvy? Who's been cheating on him all her life, and who's probably in bed with a bloke now?'

'That's enough!'

'I don't care! You're all in a tale to do for Freddy. He didn't deserve a wife like Livvy, and he's innocent, I tell you, innocent.'

'You know him better than she does?'

'Yes!'

'You slut!' Reason roared.

'I don't care. I don't care. Let the world know. I love Freddy!' And she threw herself down on the settee, beat it with her fists and sobbed.

'And these are my children,' Reason raved. 'I brought them up, gave them life. Why did I live to see this? Better if I'd been buried along with Marie.'

Gabrielle tried to say something, but failed.

'Daddy, I want him, I want him!' Susan Strickland sobbed.

'She wants – she wants. The whole story.'

'I love Freddy. I love him.'

78

She choked her sobs and sat up again.

'Daddy, listen! She didn't deserve him. There weren't any secrets from me. She was unfaithful from the start.'

'No more – I'll hear no more!'

'But I'm not to blame, and I must tell you! I pitied him, he didn't seem to know, Livvy had got him under her thumb. She was always so grand, and the poor lamb worshipped her, treated her as though she were a queen. And all the while she was out at fast parties and tumbling into bed with whoever would have her.'

'Must I listen?' Reason snarled. 'And you, you tramp, were laying for him.'

'I swear I wasn't. Freddy barely noticed me. All he could see was his precious Livvy. And anyway, I was married to Rollo, just as though that mattered to anyone. And afterwards, after Rollo, well, Freddy's eyes were beginning to open. He suspected one or two of her yuppie friends, those she was always seen around with.'

I said: 'Would those friends have names?'

Susan Strickland hesitated, gave me a narrow look. 'No. Just christian names. Livvy didn't condescend to introductions.'

'Aha,' Gabrielle said. 'A blond young man with blue eyes and smiles and nice manners. He is one?'

'That sounds like Garry. But don't ask me anything else about him.'

I asked: 'Does he drive a red Porsche?' – but Susan Strickland had turned back to her father. She had shifted a little down the settee, was pushing an appealing face towards his.

'Daddy, I never did try to seduce Freddy. He's much too loyal, he wouldn't have let me. But I love him. And that's how I know that all this is a terrible mistake. You'll do something, won't you? Please? Please? I'll never ask you for anything more in my life.'

79

Reason stared at her for a long time, his shaggy brows drawn together. Then he said, very softly:

'A mistake, is it? Ask the man who's sitting over there.'

'Daddy . . . ?'

'Tell her!' Reason thundered. 'Tell her what you told me. Tell her that, with or without a confession, some time today you're going to charge him.'

'Daddy!'

'Tell the slut.'

I said: 'I regret the evidence makes it inevitable.'

Her eyes exploded at me. 'But the evidence is faked! You put that stuff in his car, you know you did.'

I shook my head.

'Yes. And if you faked the evidence you can unfake it. Daddy has only to wave his wand and you'll jump as far and as high as he asks you.'

'No, Mrs Strickland.'

'Oh, yes. You can be bought like all the rest of them. Oh, you can make like you're incorruptible, but that's only because daddy hasn't greased your palm yet.'

'Shut your vile mouth!' Reason barked. 'There was blood on his car – was that a fake?'

'Blood on the car.' Her eyes were starting. 'Then you paid them to do it – you, you!'

'Silence, you viper!'

'You paid them – you. All on account of sainted Ginny. You saw a chance to get back at Livvy, and poor Freddy was bought and sold from that moment.'

'Hellcat!'

'You could have done it yourself.'

Reason sprang up. 'Get her out of here!'

I said: 'You'd best leave, Mrs Strickland.' Susan Strickland had sprung up too. She hissed:

'Daddy, you can't go through with this. I don't want money, you can keep your money. I want Freddy. Give me Freddy!'

'Out – out – out!'

'Give me Freddy. Just Freddy.'

'Freddy is where he belongs, hellcat, and if money buys anything, where he'll stay.'

She gave an animal scream, threw herself at him, raked her nails down the reddened cheeks. I grabbed her and hauled her away, screaming, struggling, spitting; dragged her from the room, ran her down the hall, thrust her outside and down the steps.

'Ah – ah – aaah!'

Her screams shattered the peaceful air of Lime Walk.

'I'll kill him. I mean it – I'll kill him!'

I slammed the door on Mrs Susan Strickland.

In the lounge, poor Gabrielle was wiping the cheeks of the shaking Reason. But just then the phone went and I returned to the hall to snatch it up.

'Yes?'

'Tanner, sir. We've got some results. A witness passing the car-park at around six-thirty. Saw a man run out with something in his hands and go to one of the cars.'

'Do they give a description?'

'Vague, sir. But such as it is it fits chummie. Tallish, medium build, dark clothes, in a big hurry. Witness was a shop assistant on her way home.'

'Could she pinpoint the time?'

'Not within minutes. She'd been shopping after she left off work. But near enough. She lives round the corner, thinks she must have been home before twenty-five to.'

I shrugged to myself. 'How is Welles taking it?'

'Think he may be feeling like a chat, sir. Shall we see you?'

'I'll be round. When I've finished holding someone's hand.'

Outside, fierce revving and complaining tyres marked the departure of Mrs Strickland. Inside, Gabrielle was

81

plying Reason with coffee, by the smell of it liberally spiked with scotch. His scarred face turned to me eagerly.

'Have they charged the devil, then?'

'Not yet.'

'Has he confessed?'

'We shall be interviewing him shortly.'

'A confession, George. Or nothing is done.'

'Drink your coffee, Monsieur Charles,' Gabrielle said. 'That bad girl has much to answer. See, I am having to hold your cup.'

Reason sipped but his lips were trembling.

'If she were not your daughter, you prosecute, ha?'

Reason groaned, and pushed the cup away. 'Ginny was my daughter. Now I have none.'

'You lie down for a little, yes?'

He didn't resist, but stretched out on the settee. Susan Strickland had done her job properly: four livid scars were etched in each cheek. Gabrielle arranged a cushion under the grey head, then drew me out of the room.

'Those daughters should be hung! But is it not possible what she is saying, that the son-in-law is innocent? This I will say for her, that she believes it, and almost I am believing it too.'

'She wishes to believe it.'

'It is not possible?'

I told her about Tanner's witness. Gabrielle listened with considering eyes, but in the end shook her head.

'I do not know. It is not so much.'

'It's the first. There'll be others.'

'My friend, these are strange people, and the money hangs over them like a cloud. Even Monsieur Charles. I think, with them, nothing so simple as it seems.'

I thought about it, then shook my head too. 'I'm afraid it's following a familiar pattern. Motive, opportunity and cast-iron evidence, and the testimony beginning to come in. Tanner has to charge him. He can't do other. Now it's gone a long way beyond family games.'

'And – if he is yet innocent?'

I shrugged. 'Just try to keep Reason under wraps.'

Gabrielle sighed. 'I will try. At worst, no more daughters shall cross our threshold.'

Outside in the street were rubber burns where Susan Strickland had made her exit. The police station wasn't far, and I decided to walk. I felt I could use the air.

6

I didn't hurry. It was a sunny Sunday morning when even the Kensington traffic seemed lazy. Bertie's Hotel looked completely deserted; at a thought I pushed through the swing doors.

'Yesterday afternoon. Were you on the desk when a lady came enquiring for Charles Reason?'

'That's right, sir. Mrs DeWitt's sister. But her father had left by then.'

'Did she ask after Mrs DeWitt?'

'She did, sir. But I'd got orders that Mrs DeWitt wasn't to be disturbed. The lady seemed vexed. She asked to see the book, like she wanted to make sure her sister had booked in.'

'Was anyone with her?'

'No sir.'

'Which way did she come in?'

'From the car-park, sir. And went out the same way. She was only here a couple of minutes.'

I too went out through the car-park, from which Welles's Rover had long since been towed away. By daylight it looked smaller, a bleak tarmac area surrounded on three sides by the blank walls of buildings. The entry was from a side street off Kensington Church Street and the building opposite appeared to be a warehouse. Even the hotel had few windows that overlooked the park:

84

Tanner had been lucky to find any witness. I went my way convinced that, short of a miracle, Frederick Welles would be charged that day.

The press were lined up outside the police station, but I went through them with a tight mouth. I found Tanner in his office with his Inspector, Pyatt, a blank-faced man with anxious eyes.

'Anything fresh?'

'Just the report from forensic, sir. Nothing you and I couldn't have told them. They're happy about the gloves, the blood didn't soak through much, likely not before chummie pulled them off.'

'Other blood on the clothes?'

Tanner shook his head. 'They reckon her hair absorbed most of the spray. It just copped the gloves and his sleeve. Latham says he only struck her the once.'

'What about the car-keys?'

'Negative. So he left the car unlocked when he went in.'

I told him about Susan Strickland: Tanner listened with a comical expression.

'She really thought the old boy would buy us off?'

'I think that was the object of her visit.'

Tanner wriggled his shoulders. 'Even money won't do it! Though a big one might make me go easy. But it's no go. Chummie is for it, and I think he knows that now. Very thoughtful he was this morning when I had a word with him over breakfast.'

'He's ready to talk?'

'That's my guess. Wonderful what a night in the cells will do for them.'

We set it up in the office, with a WPC stenographer at Tanner's elbow. Welles was dressed this morning in a grey lounge suit *sans* tie and *sans* shoe-laces. He shuffled in looking at no one and was ushered to a chair before the desk. The bruised eyes said he hadn't slept much, the grey cheeks that he hadn't shaved. Tanner gave him the formal warning; nothing registered in the glassy eyes. Then Tanner said, quite casually:

'Of course, you did kill her. Didn't you?'

'I – no!'

Tanner clicked his tongue. 'Let's get it over and cut the grief! Then, when Mary's got your statement, we'll see about a visit from your wife.'

'Livvy – is she here?'

'Who do you think brought your clothes?'

'But is she here?'

'We can soon fetch her. But first we shall have to have that statement.'

He stared at Tanner, then at me. 'I don't want to see Livvy,' he said. 'Not yet. Perhaps never. Just my solicitor. Just him.'

'You'll see him,' Tanner said. 'That's fine. We'll get in touch with him straightaway. You just tell us, give us your side, help us to square up the paperwork.'

He stared some more, then shook his head.

'Come on now,' Tanner said. 'You can do it. Mary here will take it all down, then she'll type it up and you can read through it. That's kosher, isn't it?'

'I won't confess!'

'Don't take it so hard,' Tanner said. 'Maybe fourteen years with remission, you could be out in nine years. What about it?'

'No!'

'Just how you got this rush of blood.'

He shook his head.

'I mean we know you did it.'

His jaw set very, very tight.

Tanner looked at me. I said:

'Welles, how did you know which room to go to?'

In his eyes, fear. I said:

86

'Because you did know. Out of forty rooms, you went straight to your sister-in-law's.'

'I rang from the desk – they told me.'

I held his gaze. 'The first time.'

'That was the first time!'

'No.'

He stared at me, mouth gaping. I said:

'You knew the number of that room before ever you came to the hotel. You knew, because you had been told. By someone who had made a point of enquiring.'

'They didn't!'

I nodded. 'Yes. On the testimony of the desk-clerk.'

'But – she didn't tell me.'

'And yet you knew?'

He was staring like an idiot. 'No . . . yes. I don't know! She said Ginny was booked into the best room. She may have mentioned the number, I don't remember, she was in such a temper at the time.'

'You admit she may have mentioned it?'

'All right – all right!'

'You were in possession of that number?'

'Yes, I may have been.'

'The number was known to you at the time you rang your father-in-law?'

'Oh God.' His body trembled. 'And that's the last nail in my coffin, is it? I knew where she was, and I made the arrangements. It couldn't have been someone else, could it?'

'Could it?'

He groaned; hugged himself.

'There, there,' Tanner said. 'No need to carry on. It didn't hurt, did it, and it's off your chest. The old rush of blood – we know all about them.'

'But it wasn't me!'

'Couldn't have been someone else . . . are you getting it all down, Mary?'

87

'I swear – I swear!'

'Easy,' Tanner said. 'Easy.'

'I was never in her room but that once.'

Tanner looked at me. I said:

'I have had a conversation with your father-in-law, Welles. He is of the fixed opinion that a second person was involved.'

His eyes clung to mine. 'Who?'

'The same person who gave you the number of the room.'

'Oh God, no!' He half-rose from the chair: Pyatt helped him sit down again. I said:

'It seems likely. It was Mrs Welles who learned that her father wasn't bankrupt, who was most urgently aware that her sister would be an obstacle to inheriting. She is also, in your father-in-law's opinion, a person of a violent and unscrupulous character, and it was she who visited the hotel and ascertained the number of Mrs DeWitt's room.'

'This is mad. Crazy!'

'Straight after which she sought a conversation with yourself, and as a result you made the arrangement that led to the death of your sister-in-law.'

'But it wasn't like that!'

'Those are facts.'

'He can't believe this. Nor can you.'

'Then what should we believe?'

'I don't know, I don't know. But he's wrong, terribly wrong. Livvy wanted to make up. She was sorry for everything. That was the whole purpose of last night.'

'I repeat, then what should we believe?'

He made the keening sound. 'Then it has to be me!'

'Is that an admission?'

'Oh God. Oh Lord.'

'It has to be him,' Tanner said. 'Have you got that, Mary?'

Welles flung his hands out towards us. 'Believe me, believe me!' he gabbled. 'I couldn't, I wouldn't have done it – not for the money, not for anything. And Livvy too, she wouldn't. There has to be another explanation. It was a thief, and he was after my car too – a thief who she surprised, and who's responsible for everything. It has to be like that, must be. And you could perhaps find him if you'd only look.'

Tanner cocked an eye at him. Shook his head.

'But someone did it!'

'Someone,' Tanner said.

'You could find him.'

'I think we have,' Tanner said. 'And never a tea-leaf showing his face.'

'So you won't – you just won't – believe me?'

'Mary doesn't either,' Tanner said.

Welles stared with agonised eyes. Then slumped in the chair, gave despairing moans. Tanner looked at me long. I said:

'Two minor points to clear up, Welles. Your wife learned that her father wasn't bankrupt from a City acquaintance. Can you tell us who that would be?'

'No I can't. She has many acquaintances.'

'But some you would know? Is there one called Garry?'

He said bitterly: 'I don't keep up with them. If you want to know about that, ask Livvy.'

I nodded 'The second point. Where should we look for your spare car-keys?'

'My spares – ?'

'A set was issued to you, wasn't it?'

'If so, then I must have lost them.'

'Perhaps you gave them to your wife?'

His look was scornful. 'She has her own car. I wouldn't let her within a mile of mine.'

'Then you can't help us?'

'No.' And his mouth snapped shut. I looked at Tanner. Tanner said:

'You've had your warning, so I won't repeat it. Frederick Michael Welles, I hereby charge you with the murder of your sister-in-law, Mrs Virgina DeWitt, at Bertie's Hotel, Kensington, at or around six-thirty p.m. on Saturday October 10th. Have you anything to say in answer to the charge?'

'I didn't do it. And you know I didn't.'

'Have you got that, Mary?' Tanner said.

'Yes sir.'

'Take him away.'

Welles was suddenly in a tremble, could scarcely rise. He seemed to want to say something, but it wouldn't come; Pyatt had practically to carry him out. The WPC took her notebook and followed.

'A pity about that, sir.' Tanner pretended a pout. 'At one time you nearly had him going. And we always like to hear chummies cough.'

I said: 'He still protects his wife.'

Tanner looked down his nose. 'Between you and me, sir, I'm glad he did. Keep it simple has always been my motto. And it's only guesswork that there's an angle.'

'Perhaps I can borrow Mary.'

Tanner mimed a double-take. 'You mean you're going to chat up the lady?'

'"Ask Livvy" was what the man said.'

Tanner stared at me soulfully. But said no more.

We drank mugs of filthy coffee. Mary came back with her typed transcript. Along with Mary I borrowed a patrol car; and, near noon, we set off for Eversley Square.

Plane trees grouped in the centre of it, overlooking impeccable flowerbeds, and the four, tall, mid-Victorian terraces had a withdrawn, remote appearance. The cars parked

there were up-market. Two nannies pushed leisurely
prams beneath the trees. Our driver stopped to make
enquiries of a third, and was directed to a house where
cherubs guarded the steps. The WPC and I mounted
them, she a sturdy girl with no-nonsense eyes, and it was
her gloved hand that pressed the bell to produce distant,
mellifluous chiming. We waited appropriately. The door
opened to reveal the lady in a silk wrap-over robe.

'Oh damn. I'm dressing for lunch. Can't you come back
this afternoon?'

I said: 'Your husband has been charged. We need to
have a few words with you, Mrs Welles.'

'Damn and damn again. Do I have to let you in?'

'I think it might be advisable.'

After a pause she stepped back from the door.

We entered a hall with a handsome staircase and period
landscapes on the walls, were led into a lofty lounge
where the furniture was painted white and decorated
with gilt. Here the pictures were Expressionist, a flavour
echoed in the jazzy carpet; overhead, a light-feature in
angular coloured-glass; on a pedestal a nymph of the
school of Henry Moore.

'So. You've bloody charged him, have you? And now
you've come to tell his grieving wife. I suppose I have to
regard myself honoured that you didn't merely pick up a
phone. Do the press know?'

'The press will be told.'

'Thanks anyway for the warning. Millionaire's wife
slain by merchant banker. When we make the news, we
certainly make it.'

She was quivering, on edge, showing a lot of figure
through the wrap-over. Drugs, drink? The brown eyes
were febrile, the wide, thin mouth on the twitch.

'Sit down, blast you. let's get on with it.'

'Were you expecting a visitor, Mrs Welles?'

91

'None of your business. And if you've come here to gloat, let me tell you you're wasting your time.'

'You will, of course, be permitted to see your husband.'

'Oh thank you so much for that. But I'm not sure I want to see him if it was really him who bashed dear Ginny. I suppose it was him?'

'He has a case to answer.'

'What a charming way to put it. The poor sod. He hadn't a chance. He should have stuck to welshing clients.'

She sprawled on a chair with a fine flash of leg. I sat. The WPC, after a moment, perched decorously on the edge of a sofa. Olivia Welles swirled her hair.

'So life goes bloody on, doesn't it. I'm the wife of a man who killed my sister. Do I need someone's permission to breathe?'

'This must be a great shock, Mrs Welles.'

'Oh I don't know. This and that.'

'You will understand that we must make full enquiries.'

'The maggot's arse bit. What else?'

I said: 'The crime was inspired, it would appear, by information you received about your father. It came from a source of yours in the city. Would you care to name that source?'

'No I wouldn't. Next question.'

I said: 'A name has been mentioned. Garry.'

Her eyes popped. 'Then I know who mentioned it. And you can tell the dirty tramp that I won't forget it.'

'Was it that man?'

'Get lost. And let me tell you something about Suzy-Lu. She's got hot pants twice over for Freddy, and she'd say anything to do me down. What else did she say?'

I shook my head.

'Come on, come on, I want to hear it! She's been putting it around for ever that I'm Belgravia's leading nympho. Isn't that it? That I'm a whore?'

92

'Your sister was in a disturbed state.'

'Oh charming. So now I'll throw a party because my old man's locked away.' She breathed fiercely, tossed her hair. 'And you can go to hell,' she said. 'I was told about daddy by a good friend who I won't have dragged into this business.'

'It might assist us, Mrs Welles.'

'I'm not telling, is that straight? I did hear about it, and that's enough, you can say I'm protecting his reputation.'

'And that was yesterday?'

Her hair swished.

'Shortly before you came seeking your father?'

Another swish.

'Accompanied, it appeared, by a fair-haired gentleman in a red Porsche?'

'You bastard.' Her eyes savaged me. 'I didn't ask him to put his oar in. And he wasn't with me. He just happened along. I do have friends who drive Porsches.'

'And he went with you to the hotel?'

'Bloody no.'

'You sought your father there alone.'

'Yes.'

'And, not finding him, made some enquiries about your sister.'

'What if I did?'

'For example, her room number.'

Her eyes were hating me. 'You sod. Of course I made enquiries about her, wouldn't anyone else have done? She'd just flown in, remember? Little Ginny from New York. If she was staying there I wanted to know. Big surprise. My own sister.'

'And you learned her room number?'

'So what's with that? I asked for the register, of course. Little miss had gone to bye-byes, I couldn't see her. But I wanted to make certain she was there.'

93

'And later, you mentioned the number to your husband?'

The brown eyes raked me for quite a while. Then the hair swung. 'Oh for Christ's sake! Let's stop horsing around, shall we? I'm with you now. Yes, all right. I may have let it slip to Freddy.'

'You can't be certain?'

'Yes and no. I was in a mood when I got back. I mean daddy playing a trick like that. You may have noticed. I blew my top.'

'But then, I understand, you calmed down.'

'I'm a bitch but I can't help it. I was mad because that little cow was over here to soft-soap daddy. I mean you know what's at stake here. We're talking in billions, not small change. And it was the principle. She was here to grab it. If I blew my top, my God I had reason.'

'And – your husband?'

'He's a banker, isn't he? Naturally, he was upset too. Money's the air that Freddy breathes, and he couldn't bear the thought of it slipping away.'

'So then you calmed down.'

'Yes. I began to see there was only one thing to do. If little Miss Innocent wasn't to get away with it, we would have to mend our fences with daddy. At first I thought I'd go myself, but Freddy said no, best if he prepared the ground, and I could see the sense in that because he's always got on well with daddy.'

'It was your husband's suggestion.'

A sweep of the hair. 'I said I was a bitch. But it's on the table.'

'And you gave him the room number?'

'Must have done. There's how many rooms he might have gone to?'

I said: 'What was his mood when he left the house?'

She seemed to think about it. 'Quiet. He hadn't got

94

very much to say. But then, he had to face up to daddy, hadn't he?'

'Was he wearing gloves?'

'Oh, I wouldn't have noticed. But he may have kept some in the car.'

'Woollen gloves?'

'Who knows? I had the TV on when he left.'

'You were watching a programme?'

'I told you that. I needed something to help settle me down. And yes, before you ask again, the programme wasn't quite over when Freddy went.'

'Making the time, say five minutes to six?'

The slightest swirl. 'It had to be that.'

'You're quite certain?'

The tips of her fingers came together. 'Yes.'

A car parked somewhere close in the square and Olivia Welles's gaze slid to the window. But nobody mounted the steps to set the harmonious chimes going. On her sofa the WPC sat gazing at the carpet with angry eyes. I said:

'And after your husband had gone?'

'What about it?'

'You still went on watching television?'

'This and that. Until I got that bloody phone call from Freddy. Then I was really knocked flat. He wanted me to get in touch with our solicitor – I mean, on a Saturday evening! As it happened I knew that Tommy Beaumont had gone to a show, a fat chance of getting in touch with him there. I just hung up and screamed my head off.'

'You had no doubt that your husband was guilty?'

'Didn't know what to think, did I? If he'd been arrested there had to be grounds, and I knew the idea of that money was riding him. It was out of character, perhaps, but these quiet people sometimes flip, and something

95

might have happened to him on the way there. Just once or twice I've seen him blow up.'

'You changed your mind later.'

'Did I?'

'At the police station.'

'Oh there.' A full swirl. 'Well, that was for daddy, who was being so beastly about poor Freddy. I couldn't let the poor fish down, and daddy could do something if he wanted.' She flickered me a look. 'You'd be surprised. Or then again perhaps you wouldn't.'

I said: 'You thought bribery was a possibility?'

'Oh God no! Let's change the subject. If Freddy did it, then that's that, and no good me giving him a character reference.'

She rose irritably, fetched a cigarette, inserted it in an elegant holder. I was supposed to light it. I didn't. Waspishly, she lit it herself with an enamelled-silver lighter.

'What will he get?'

I shrugged. 'May we go back to your movements yesterday?'

'What movements?'

I said: 'Say during the two hours between your husband' ringing your father, and his leaving the house?'

'You go to hell.'

I said: 'Did you remain here?'

'And I said you could go to hell. I've told you all you need to know, and my private life belongs to me.'

'We can ask your husband.'

Her eyes were furious. 'Perhaps you've already asked him.'

'Perhaps.'

'Then why ask me? If you care to believe a word he says.'

'I would like your account.'

'Oh sod it.' The holder wobbled as she dragged on it.

'If you must know I took off. I wasn't in the mood to sit around in houses.'

'Where did you go?'

'Christ knows. I took the car and drove around.'

'Drove where?'

'Not to bloody Kensington. Not to see my dear sister or my dear daddy.'

'Then where?'

'I don't know where! Just around. To let off steam.'

'Did you call anywhere?'

'Sodding no. I wasn't in the mood to make small-talk.'

I said: 'For two hours?'

'It wasn't two hours! I was back here when Freddy left, remember?'

I said: 'And if he denies that?'

'Then you'll have to choose between his word and mine.'

She dragged savagely, drilling smoke. The WPC was examining her nails. I said:

'Without wishing to question your account, I would feel happier if it could be confirmed.'

'Oh bugger.' She took a huge drag. 'So I'm the nympho of Belgravia. Will that do? Tom, Dick or Harry, it doesn't matter who when I'm upset. You'll like that. It fits my character. And little Miss Innocence here is loving it. But don't think I'll name the toy-boy, even if I remember who it was.'

'You visited some man?'

'Oh, you're lovely. Yes I visited a man. And he'll remember, don't you worry. Probably hasn't got over it yet.'

'But – you won't name him?'

'No, you bastard. I told you, my private life's my own.'

'And you were back watching television at five minutes to six?'

'Before that too.' She dragged. 'Ask Freddy.'

97

'We shall ask him.'

'Yes, just won't you.' She drilled smoke over my head. 'But why does it matter anyway, and why am I getting the third degree?'

I shook my head.

'I'm the injured party. It's my old man who's sitting in a cell. A little more sympathy wouldn't come amiss, especially from one of daddy's friends. You are his friend, aren't you?'

I watched her.

'And I'm his daughter – whatever he thinks of me! And Ginny's sister. Oh I know I'm a bitch, but even I am human too.'

I shrugged, and got to my feet; the WPC got to hers. I said:

'We shall need a statement from you, Mrs Welles. Perhaps you will arrange to visit Kensington police station.'

'When I've seen Tom Beaumont. Not before.'

I inclined my head. 'One other small thing. The spare keys to your husband's car – would you happen to know where they were?'

'No I wouldn't.' Now she jumped up, scrubbed out the cigarette in an ashtray. 'And the next time you bastards come visiting, perhaps you'll have the manners to give me a ring first.'

She followed us to the door; she slammed it after us.

'She was lying, sir!' the WPC said. 'I'll swear she wasn't there when her husband left. She's just trying to push him in a little deeper.'

Yes; but my attention was elsewhere; on a car parked a few spaces down the pavement. A red Porsche 924S, it had standing beside it a hefty young man with blond hair. Who peeled off when he saw us emerge, and came smilingly to meet us at the foot of the steps.

7

He advanced his hand; I ignored it. That didn't alter his winning smile. He said:

'I'm Garry Maiden, sir. We met yesterday. I was completely stunned when I heard what had happened. I would very much like to have a few words, since I'm afraid you may be thinking that I'm to blame.'

Six foot or a shade over, in a baggy blue blouson and baggy pants; an athletic presence suggesting gyms and squash courts; tanned oval features with a bold jaw. I said:

'You are here to visit Mrs Welles?'

'Well, to offer my support! She sounded quite frantic on the phone, so I jumped in the Porsche and came over.' He put the smile away. 'Is she completely gaga?'

'Mrs Welles is naturally disturbed.'

He nodded. 'You saw her yesterday, and now this frightful thing has happened, with poor old Freddy in a cell. You went easy on her, did you?'

I said nothing. I had my back to the Welles house, but the WPC was watching it avidly. Quite certainly, Mrs Welles was observing the scene at the foot of her steps.

'Was she able to help you at all?'

I said: 'If you have anything to tell me, perhaps you will accompany me to Kensington police station.'

'Oh dear, that sounds serious! Of course, I'll do anything you say. But I thought . . . well, a few words. And Bogey's Bar is just round the corner.'

'Bogey's Bar . . . ?'

'We could have a bite there. Then I could visit the lady later. She didn't specifically ask me round, but I feel I must do what I can.'

'Weren't you taking her to lunch?'

'What? No! That is, I would have if she'd asked me. Only, on the phone, she didn't sound like someone who was thinking about food.'

Then I did look back towards the house. Olivia Welles was standing at the window. She was staring down with hating eyes, especially at Maiden, who kept his face averted. I shrugged deliberately.

'How far away is this bar?'

'Not two hundred yards. It's fun, you'll like it.'

So I dismissed the WPC and the car.

From her window, Olivia Welles watched the pair of us out of sight.

The first thing that met you in Bogey's Bar was a larger-than-life picture of Humphrey Bogart, and if the muzak wasn't playing *As Time Goes By* it was playing something else that nearly resembled it. There were other pictures and cartoons of Bogart and of Katherine Hepburn, Lauren Bacall and the like, and a huge blow-up of Ingrid Bergman urging Sam to Play It. The bar was noisy with yuppies and their girl friends. Most of them seemed to know Maiden. A raven-haired young man sporting flyaway lapels implored him to introduce his quadrangular friend. Smilingly, Maiden pushed his way through, led us to the quiet end of the bar. There was an area of tables and chairs where a waitress was serving food.

'What will you have? They don't stock bitter.'

A couple of lagers it had to be.

'A ploughman's?'

I chose a table with a view down the bar. Maiden fetched the straw-flavoured liquor. I lit a pipe, left mine untouched.

'Sorry about the noise. Bogey's is the in-thing.'

'Who are your friends down the room?'

'City-types to a man.'

'Is Mrs Welles an *habituee*?'

'Olivia, yes. Or was till now.'

'And her husband?'

'Never seen him here. This wouldn't be Freddy Welles's taste.'

'She came alone?'

'Or one of us brought her. Are you asking if she has a special friend?'

'Has she?'

His smile was thornproof. 'If I knew, would you expect me to tell you?'

I looked at him. He drank lager. The waitress dumped our two ploughman's. Maiden scribbled on her pad. He drank some more lager. He said:

'So she plays the field. She isn't alone. That's the form in this year of grace. And she's probably told you so herself, if I know anything about Olivia. She's never hidden it. And I suspect her husband knows it, thinks it best to play along.'

'So nobody special?'

'One or another.'

'I'm not asking this for fun.'

'Then take your pick.'

He nodded down the bar, where he of the flyaways was juggling bread rolls, another was balancing a glass on his head, a third flicking peanuts at selected targets. I smoked. Maiden drank. Now the muzak *was* playing *As Time Goes By*. I said:

101

'So you've something to tell me.'

'Yes. And it isn't easy.'

'Let me help you. It was you who blew the gaff on the lady's father.'

'Yes.' He wasn't smiling now. 'I thought I was being a clever boy. I'm a market-maker, you understand, Tonks and Leman, Old Broad Street. Well, I had confidential information which set me milking the computers, and after the umpteenth check I was sure that Reason was still in business. Allgemein Zurich. It only sounds Swiss. Actually a British-controlled nominee company. And the read-outs I was getting were fabulous, they made even Nomura look modest.'

'You could be certain that Reason was behind it?'

'Yes. As I said, I had information. And Reason had always been a mystery, the way he seemed to fold after Big Bang. So then I knew. He wasn't down. He was one of the biggest players in the game. And Olivia and Suzy, that's the other daughter, still treating him like a case of mumps. So what was I to do? I mean, Olivia's a friend, I couldn't go on watching her cut her own throat. She could become the richest woman in the world. A million is small change to Allgemein Zurich.'

'And yesterday you told her.'

He nodded. 'I tried to make it a gentle hint, that her father wasn't quite on the bottom and that it might be worth her while to sweeten him. But you know Olivia, she wasn't happy with that, in the end I had to tell her what I knew. And she blew her top, tried to phone him, then got in her car and drove over there.'

'With you behind her.'

'What was I to do? In that sort of mood she was capable of anything. I could only pray that she wouldn't find him, and of course, as you know, she didn't.' He swigged lager. 'Yes, I know I'm to blame! But I couldn't guess what was going to happen. It doesn't help, though. I still feel responsible. It's all because I opened my big mouth.'

'Yet you knew you were dealing with an unstable character.'

'He hung his head. 'Yes. Rub it in.'

'You could as well have dropped a hint to her husband.'

'I know, I know. I'm a stupid bastard.'

After a moment he swallowed off the lager, then jumped up to fetch more. At the bar he had to fend off a discharge of peanuts and raucous invitations from his friends for him to join them. So the smile was back when he returned, still with a peanut in the blond hair. He settled, sipped, nibbled some cheese, gave me a little, placating look.

'They're not so bad. You have to know them. They're under pressure all the week.'

'Market-makers?'

'For today. Some will be fund-managers tomorrow.'

Lager was flushing his fair complexion and he stuffed more food into his mouth. I didn't eat, didn't drink, sat puffing and staring over his head. At last he said:

'It was learning that her sister was over here that really did it. The youngest one, I mean, the poor kid who's dead. That sent her mad. She stormed off to the hotel. I didn't dare go in with her. But her father had left and the sister gone to bed, and the hotel people wouldn't let Livvy disturb her. She came out speechless, drove back here like crazy, went in and made a scene with her old man.'

'With you still tagging along?'

'I had to. I was afraid what she might do. You said it yourself, she can be unstable, though mostly she's a wonderful person. And then, at the house, she dragged me in with her to tell Freddy what I knew. Heaven knows I didn't want to, but I wasn't given the option.'

I said: 'We have interrogated Welles. He makes no mention of your presence at that time.'

'No. And that's not surprising.'

'Not . . . ?'

Maiden shook his head and drank lager.

He said: 'So I'm a bastard. That's established. But even bastards have to draw a line somewhere. And both these people are friends of mine, however weird that may strike you. I know Livvy better than Freddy, period, but I still like old Freddy. And I won't say anything to prejudice his chances. That's supposing he still has some.'

I didn't say anything.

Maiden said: 'Has he?'

I said: 'Welles was charged this morning.'

'Oh dear! Does that mean . . . ?'

'It means that your friend has a case to answer.'

'But . . . what sort of case?'

I said: 'Sufficient.'

'Are you telling me you've got him?'

I didn't tell him anything, just struck a fresh light for my pipe. Maiden gazed at his plate, then at me.

'And that's why you've just been round to Livvy's! Oh dear, oh dear. And she, poor soul, with nobody there to lean on.'

'It follows that she had to know.'

'She must be absolutely shattered. How did she take it?'

I shrugged, stared over his head at a Bogey picture.

'Then it's really true?' Maiden plunged for his lager.

I said: 'Have you something more to tell me?'

'I don't know. I mean all this time . . . are you sure there hasn't been a mistake?'

'No mistake.'

'Well, I don't know.'

'If you have information it's your duty to tell me.'

He drank, fiddled with his plate, glanced down the bar

104

at his playful colleagues. They were playing boule with the bread rolls, their mark a small bundle of bank notes.

'And he didn't mention me?'

I puffed.

'He wouldn't. He'd be hoping you wouldn't get on to me. Not that I can tell you very much either. It's really a question of how it's taken.'

'So.'

'Well, Livvy was seething, and so was Freddy when he heard the tale – not with his father-in-law, but with her, because she'd probably queered their pitch. Then he wanted chapter and verse from me, whether they could be certain I'd got it right, and of course I had, and I proved it to him, because he knew very well . . . never mind!'

'That you had confidential information?'

'All that's neither here nor there. The fact was he knew I was right and that his father-in-law was a billionaire. What he had to do then was to put things right, and that wasn't going to be so easy. Livvy had been offhand with her father, and the youngest daughter was right there, buttering him up. Old Freddy stomped up and down for a while and Livvy had quietened off too. She wanted him to invite her father to the house, but Freddy couldn't see any percentage in that. In the end he rang his father-in-law and managed to soft-talk him into a meeting, said there'd been misunderstandings on both sides, that he would apologise and explain.'

I said: 'I was at Reason's and heard that call.'

Maiden paused. 'Then you know what I'm saying is right! Freddy rang him, fixed it up to meet in Bertie's at six-thirty.'

He drank, I puffed.

'And that's all?'

'No. Now I've got to be a real bastard.'

'I've heard nothing very damning yet.'

105

He gave me a blue stare.

'When he'd hung up, Livvy was swearing that it wouldn't do any good, not with Miss Sweet-puss hanging around and putting on her act of eternal devotion. Old Freddy looked at her for a bit, and then said this: "That can change", and when she asked him what he meant he wouldn't give her an answer.'

'Nothing else?'

'Isn't that enough?'

I shrugged at Bogey on the wall. 'He may only have been thinking that Mrs DeWitt's stay wouldn't be a long one.'

'But that wasn't how he said it!'

'How did he say it?'

'I don't know. But it wasn't a throwaway. And if he really was the one who did it, then I would have thought it had some significance.' He stared some more. 'You weren't fooling me, were you? Freddy was really charged this morning?'

'He was charged.'

'Then all right. I've said my piece, and it's off my conscience.'

He jammed food in his mouth. He seemed disappointed. I said:

'Where do I find you if I need a statement?'

After a moment, he fished out a card. And I laid down a note beside my untouched glass.

But the pantomime wasn't over yet. As I rose from the table the swing-doors to the street were crashed back violently: into the bar strode Susan Strickland to stand glaring at the Hooray Henrys. Their uproar faded: almost eerily the muzak's *Night and Day* swelled in the background. Her blazing eyes went from one to another, fastened finally on the flyaway lapels.

'Nick. You did it – you killed my sister!'

Flyaway's eyes couldn't have opened wider.

'Yes – you did it. You're Livvy's cat's-paw! She laid it on, but Nicky did it.'

'You – you.' He was gaping. 'You're high as a kite, Suzy!'

'Oh no I'm not. I'm more sober than you. And you're the little boy who jumps when she tells you. And you jumped round to Kensington and killed my sister.'

'Killed who – ?'

'My sister Ginny!'

'But your sister Ginny lives in New York.'

'Only she was here. In Bertie's Hotel. Where Livvy sent you last night to kill her.'

'You're high, Suzy. Right up there.'

'You killed her, and then you framed poor Freddy! But it won't work, Nicky. I'm going to the police. I'll never let you get away with this.'

He went on staring aghast, this black-haired young man with a long, narrow, flushed face, with his mates eyeing him, eyeing Susan Strickland, and the hiatus filled only by drooling muzak. But then his face changed, the eyes came to life, and suddenly he threw back his head and laughed.

'You're gorgeous, Suzy. Gorgeous! For a moment there you had me going.'

'Yes, laugh, you bastard. But it won't help you.'

'Gorgeous! What would we do without her?'

'I'm going to the police.'

'Of course, of course. It's worth bubbly. Set them up, Sam.'

'They'll get you.'

'The Bollinger, Sam. And just as it was turning out another bloody Sunday!'

Her eyes snapped. On a table near her was somebody's unfinished drink. She snatched it up and discharged it in the young man's grinning face.

'Take that, you murdering bastard!'

'That . . . wasn't necessary!'

'Perhaps now you'll realise I mean business. They've just charged Freddy, do you know that? But they're never, never going to get away with it.'

'But . . . it can't be true?' He scrubbed at his face: Susan Strickland took a step closer.

'So last night where were you, Nicky, between six and six-thirty? Where were you?'

'Where . . . ? I'd been to Twickers, you lunatic.'

'Oh yes. With fifty thousand others.'

'But Nigel was there. And Kevin and Jake.'

'So you're all in it. It's a conspiracy!'

'Suzy, you're crazy.'

'If you didn't kill her, then one of you other bastards did.' She glared round at the flushed faces, at the gimlet eyes of the women. 'You'd do it, wouldn't you? Any of you. With money like that egging you on. Livvy could buy and sell all of you with what my father will leave behind.' She spat, by chance in the direction of the little bundle of notes on the floor. 'Only you're fools, do you know that? Because clever Livvy may not get it. And that leaves me, do you hear? Me, with the millions at my elbow. And I'll pay twice what Livvy's paying – that's the deal, you charming people! Twice, twice. To give me the killer. To put that bastard on the spot. So think about it. My father's old. And I'm doubling the money for Freddy's ransom.'

Beside me Maiden stirred. 'Shouldn't you do something about this!'

I said: 'Why? She's offering a reward. It may be irregular, but it isn't illegal.'

'But with that sort of money – she could buy false witness.'

'I think you may leave us to sort that out.'

'I don't know . . . I mean even you.'

I gave him a look that shut him up. Meanwhile there was a buzz among the yuppies and several close conversations going on: they didn't include the young man, Nick, who was standing alone, still dabbing his face. For her part, Susan Strickland had turned her back on them and was ordering a drink at the bar. When she'd got it she lit a cigarette and perfumed a blow-up of Lauren Bacall. Finally a shock-headed fellow detached himself from the group and sidled up to the bar.

'Suzy-Lu . . . this wouldn't be a con-game?'

She gave him a flashing eyes-over.

'I mean, if it's true about your sister, and if the Bill have busted Livvy's husband . . .'

Susan Strickland made the gesture of feeling money.

'No, but I mean! You could be right. Some of them here are mad enough. And they'd do anything for Livvy.'

'Wouldn't you, Jake?'

'No, but listen! The Bill may get to thinking like you. So then we'd best get our tales straight, see whose neck is really sticking out. And I'm in the clear. I was at Twickers. Only we broke up after the game. And if you've really got something on . . . someone, well, he'd have had time to get over to Bertie's.'

Susan Strickland blew smoke in his face. 'Along with you. And Nigel. And Kevin.'

'No, I went straight home!'

'No good, Jacko. I want him at Bertie's or no deal.'

'He was heading that way . . .'

'Bertie's, Jacko. Or are you just covering for yourself?'

Jake, Jacko peeled off again, slid back to compare notes with his friends. At my elbow, Maiden bolted some cheese, cast a wistful eye at my untouched glass.

'You can see what will happen . . .'

'Hush!'

'They're going to sell out some unlucky sod. And I

could tell them it's a waste of time, just making grief for the poor bastard.'

'Here comes another.'

'That's Kevin. One of Livvy's has-beens from way back.'

This one was clad in a lively check and sported a tie on which was printed a nude. He had a young-old face and his ginger hair was brushed up in a style. But he never really got going, just a bit about Kensington on his way home; then the circus was interrupted again: and this time by Olivia Welles.

I heard Maiden gasp as she walked in, and certainly the only other sound was the muzak. Like royalty, she paused after making her entrance, but the expression on her face was not a royal smile. I kept my eye on Susan Strickland. She had jerked upright, away from the bar. But Olivia Welles ignored her. Ignored the yuppies. Strode straight up the gangway to where we were sitting. And now the gasp came from Susan Strickland, who had spotted me for the first time. Olivia Welles towered over our table. The brown eyes were boring into Maiden. Then, very casually, she shifted the vanity-bag she was carrying from her right hand to her left, and struck the unhappy Maiden two smart blows across the face.

'Traitor!'

'Livvy, that wasn't fair!'

'Traitor! I saw you making up to this louse.'

'But Livvy, I had to – '

'Making up to him! You could have stayed clear, but you thrust yourself forward. What a friend. Judas Iscariot. And not even thirty pieces of silver.'

'Livvy, don't get in a rage – '

'Not get in a rage, you turncoat scab! What sort of tales have you been telling him, what lies, what wicked inventions?'

'Livvy, he saw me with you yesterday. I felt responsible, I had to tell him – '

'Ha, ha, responsible! The man's conscience pricked him. He had to go babbling to the police. And what else did this smart-alick here get out of you – what else – what else? It wouldn't stop at that.'

'Well – '

'Go on! He saw you go off with me. He'd want to know what happened after that, wouldn't he?'

'Livvy, please – !'

'How I went to the hotel and made enquiries about my dear sister – how you followed me home – how you told Freddy – and how Freddy reacted! He'd want to know that.'

'But it was nothing – it didn't help him!'

'You fool. He's the best in the game. I know, because he's just turned me over, made me say a dozen things I should have kept quiet. And you, you innocent, you'd have been putty, he'd have squeezed you till your eyes popped. And you'd never have known. You'll have damned Freddy and think you've just been passing the time of day.'

'But I didn't – !'

'You make me puke. And you're my big friend, the one I can trust.'

And now Bogey's Bar began quietly to empty, as the goggling yuppies learned the score. They stopped not upon the order, but softly and silently faded through the doors. Perhaps I should have tried to stop them, they might have known something; but as it was I let them go. Now, excluding Sam, we were four; because Susan Strickland had slowly edged closer. And the face she was turning on Maiden wasn't friendly, was the face that preceded raking claws.

'You – bastard! You filthy pig!'

'Hold it!' I said. 'None of that, Mrs Strickland.'

'He's been lying to you. Lying about Freddy! When he knows all the time that Freddy didn't do it.'

'Just keep calm.'

'He knows – he knows. It was one of that gang who've just gone out. And I'd have found out who, too – while all the time he was selling Freddy down the river!'

'Stay back, Mrs Strickland.'

Now she'd edged too close, and Maiden was belatedly getting to his feet. Her hands shot out – but then she went staggering, sent flying among the chairs by a sisterly clout.

'Bitch! Bitch! Bitch!'

'Take yourself out of here!' Olivia Welles snarled. 'I know your game, my little miss, and it isn't on, so don't think it.'

'You hate Freddy!'

'Out. Out.'

'It's you who's behind this – you, you!'

'I'll break your arm for you, you bitch.'

'I know it. I know it. And I'll prove it!'

I was on my feet too. Olivia Welles moved threateningly towards her sister. But in a moment Susan Strickland had overturned a chair between them and was making her escape to the doors. There she paused for a Pythian shot.

'Murdering bitch. Murderess! Murderess!'

A determined motion by Olivia Welles sent her scuttling into the street.

'The slanderous little cow.' She returned a few paces to savage us with her eyes. 'A treacherous friend and a foulmouthed sister. I'm doing well for one morning, aren't I?'

Maiden was trying to get the smile going. 'You don't mean all this, Livvy, you know you don't.'

'Don't I? You'll find so, my man. A friend of mine only lets me down once.'

'This business is getting to all of us.'

'You're out, Garry Maiden. Out. And so is that crew

112

who left us so suddenly. They've had their day with Olivia Welles.' She turned to me. 'So play your tricks, little man. Get all the dirt you can from my ex-friends. They're yours to keep. Like this shit here. And just in passing, they all smoke pot.'

'Livvy!'

Her smile was tigerish. 'Goodbye, Garry. You served your turn.'

'But Livvy, you can't – '

'Goodbye. Goodbye. I would say thanks for the memory, but I can't.'

Did she really wink . . . ? I couldn't be certain. Her hair swished grandly, and she turned away: made a royal progress down the bar and pressed a wing-door open with one finger.

'I'm going after her!'

'Don't bother.'

'But in that mood – you don't understand!'

'Leave it,' I said. 'It was a nice scene. I thought the lady played it well.'

I got the blue stare. 'Well, perhaps you're right.' He sank down again on his chair. But now the sight of my glass became irresistible and he grabbed it and began gulping. I picked up my pipe. The muzak had got itself back to *As Time Goes By*. Sam was making a pretence of washing glasses. I saluted Bogey on the wall and left.

Sometimes, just sometimes, when you want a cab one hauls up at your very feet. It did then. I told the driver Kensington. Which was the address on the card Garry Maiden had given me.

8

I had the driver drop me at Bertie's Hotel, where they had a framed street-map hanging in reception. The bar there was lively with our local gang of yuppies, but though I longed for a drink I didn't linger to observe them. Cars packed the park. I hurried through them and into the shabby side-street, paused to check my watch, then set off on the route I'd traced on the street-map. Kendal Terrace was where Maiden lived. I made it just six minutes from the car-park. Another pleasant Victorian backwater, though not yet, the cars said, a yuppie haven. Fords, Jappos obstructed the pavements along with occasional Volvos and Audis, while some of the house-fronts were tatty and in need of fresh paint. I strolled along to forty-four. The houses there were in good nick. Forty-four comprised four flats of which Maiden's occupied the first floor. I went up the steps, examined the name-plates, from the corner of my eye saw a curtain move. The name that went with it was a Mrs H. Brackley. I pressed the button and waited.

'Ye-es?'

The lady who answered was a dashing, well-painted fifty, clad in a short-skirted purple dress that revealed a great deal of unappetising leg.

'Mrs Brackley?'

She simpered. 'Call me Henrietta, darling. Should I know you?'

I said: 'Police,' and flashed my warrant.

'Oh.' She looked thoughtful for a moment. 'But never mind, darling, you can't help it. And I was just going to pour myself a little drinkie. You will come in and share it, won't you?'

I said: 'I am seeking information.'

'But of course, darling, what else? So come in and brighten my life. Handsome policemen we don't often see here.'

She backed off and I went in, catching a whiff of carnation as I passed her. She showed me into a small lounge with foam-backed curtains and Homeplan furniture. The latter included a well-stocked bar. She went to it and set up glasses. A gin-and-orange was thrust into my hand: I wasn't being lucky with drinks that day.

'Drink up, darling. You're not local, are you?'

'If you don't mind, Mrs Brackley – '

'Mind, darling? This is making my day. Ask me all the lovely questions you can think of.'

'These are purely routine enquiries. They concern the tenant in the flat above this one. Would he be an acquaintance?'

She sighed. 'Dear Garry? No. Though of course I dote on the beautiful creature.' She swept me with her eyes. 'What's he done?'

'Just routine. Does he have many visitors?'

'Of course – what do you expect? With a body like that. And those eyes.'

'He has women visitors?'

'You darling man.'

'Perhaps one in particular?'

'Don't they always.'

'Then you can describe her?'

She nodded teasingly. 'But not till you've told me what it's about.'

I stared into the painted eyes. 'Very well. A woman

died last night in Bertie's Hotel. This morning a man was charged with her murder. My questions relate to that investigation.'

She went still, the drink poised.

'You're not telling me that – it was Garry?'

'Another man has been charged.'

'Another man.'

'But Maiden is involved in the investigation.'

Mrs Brackley sat, her gawky legs sprawled, and placed her glass down beside her.

'And I thought I was in luck,' she said sourly. 'Handsome You come ringing my bell, darling. Was she the woman?'

'No.'

'But she's all tied up with it?'

'If she is who I suppose.'

'And she's dragged Garry in along with her – yes, I can believe it. She looked a dangerous mare if ever I saw one.'

'Then perhaps you will describe her.'

'Why not?' The eyes she fixed on me were mean. 'A tall bitch with strawberry-blonde hair and brown eyes that look at people like they were dirt. Would she be the one?'

'Go on.'

'Wears jingly ear-rings and the latest clothes. Drives a cream BMW and doesn't give a damn where she parks it.'

'Do you know her name?'

'No. But I knew she was trouble for someone, darling. And it had to be him. Oh Gawd, why are you men such bloody fools?'

'Was she here often?'

'Two or three times a week.'

'How long had it gone on?'

'Since Easter anyway.'

'In your view, a strong attachment?'

116

'On his side. I can't speak for hers. Just her toy-boy, like as not, and him too starry-eyed to see it.'

'He was under her influence?'

'I keep telling you. So what has she let him in for, darling?'

I shrugged, and trying to keep it casual, said: 'Was she by any chance here yesterday?'

Mrs Brackley's eyes were sharp. 'Now we're really getting to it, aren't we?' she said.

'Well?'

'About five p.m. He hadn't been in himself very long. Something after four was when he got back, and she waltzed in an hour later.'

I said: 'Can you be sure of those times?'

'Yes, darling. I was watching the snooker. Steve Davis was on when Garry came back, then at five I had to switch channels. She got here about then. And Steve Davis came on at four.'

It sounded kosher. 'How long was she here?'

Mrs Brackley gave it thought. 'A couple of hours at the outside, it wasn't her usual form at all. I reckoned they'd quarrelled – not that that was unusual, I'd heard them having words before – but this time it must have gone too far, because Garry took off and left her up there.'

'He left her in the flat?'

'That's what I'm saying. Took off for a spell, to cool down. He came back about half-an-hour later, but her car had gone soon after that.'

I said: 'Can you time those movements?'

'Around six, I should think, when he took off. And her car was gone before seven, so she didn't waste much time after he got back.'

'You could swear to six?'

A flicker in her eye. 'Near enough, darling. If that's what you want.'

'But can you?'

117

'You'll have to take my word. I wasn't holding a stop-watch on them.'

I said: 'This may be very important. Try to think what you were doing when you saw him go out.'

'I was boiling an egg for my tea, darling, but that's all I can tell you. Around six.'

And I had to leave it at that. Steve won his match, and Mrs Brackley went through to get her tea. She'd heard feet running down the stairs and had returned to her lounge in time to see Maiden depart along Kendal Terrace. Around six. Going towards Church Street. While the BMW remained misparked outside. Intrigued, she'd taken tea in the lounge, and had seen him return half-an-hour later; but then she'd gone through to wash up, and so had missed the departure of Olivia Welles. Back and forth, that was the story. Fuelled with sips of gin-and-orange. At last, I took a token sip of mine.

'You have been very helpful, Mrs Brackley. We shall need a written statement from you. I'll arrange for a car to take you to the police station.'

'Oh Gawd, do I have to do that?'

'You have given us important information.'

'I haven't done for him, have I?'

'Naturally, we shall have to investigate what you have told us.'

'He's such an innocent, the poor so-and-so, him with his blue eyes and his Porsche. And always a smile for everyone. I can't believe he's done anything very wrong. You did say you had the bloke who did it?'

'A man has been charged with the crime.'

'Well then, it can't be as bad as all that. Could be that old Garry's in the clear after all.'

I shrugged. 'Could be.'

'Yes. It could. And anyway, it brought me a handsome copper.' She wafted the carnation close. 'Do you have to rush off so soon, darling?'

118

I made her a grin. 'Was it tough in the chorus?'

'Cheeky. I've played in panto, too.'

Susan Strickland was in police station reception and she jumped up when I entered.

'Please. You've got to let me see Freddy! I'm the only friend he has in the world.'

'I'm sorry, Mrs Strickland.'

'But there's nobody else. Rotten Livvy will never see him. And daddy's against him. They're all against him. He's only got me left.'

'Perhaps later. If he wishes to see you.'

She burst into tears. 'Tell him. Tell him I love him and know that he's innocent, that he isn't alone, will never be alone!'

The WPC, Mary, hastened forward to lead Susan Strickland back to a chair. To me she said:

'We've got another witness, sir. A man who works for the local council. He was passing the hotel car-park at something after six last evening.'

'What did he see?'

'He saw a man in the park, sir. He was standing near a car and had something in his hand. Then, when he noticed witness, he concealed whatever it was in his hand, and witness saw him turn and start to walk towards the hotel.'

'Could he give a description?'

'Tall, dark clothing. And the car was parked where we found Welles's, sir.'

'And the time?'

'He wasn't too sure. Puts it at ten minutes or a quarter-past six.'

I went on through, to find Tanner on the phone; he gave me a big wink and motioned to a chair. I sat down, filled my pipe, listened to a conversation that was largely monosyllabic. Finally he hung up and rubbed his large hands.

'Right, sir! We're getting the act together. Mary told me you didn't get far with Welles's missus, but now we don't need her for when chummie left the house.'

I grunted. 'Just as well! I can place her somewhere else at that time.'

'You mean the lady lied to us?'

'We'll come to that. Let's hear what you've just had in.'

Tanner leered at me. 'The word of a judge – and you can't get very much better than that, sir! Judge Levison. He's a neighbour of theirs, plays bridge and that sort of caper. Well, he was putting his car away in the mews just as Welles was collecting his, and he knows the time because he'd promised his missus that he'd be home by six p.m.'

'And he was on time?'

'Five minutes to spare, sir. Welles left his house at five minutes to six. Which fits to a T. Because we've got a witness who saw him entering the hotel at six-fifteen, with the weapon in his hand. It wouldn't take long to do a job like that, sir, bash the girl, muss the room, grab the loot. Then ten minutes later our shop-girl is seeing him dumping the gear in his car. Wouldn't you say that tied it up?'

'It would. If the man was Welles.'

'Oh, come on, sir,' Tanner said. 'Miracles is what we do not believe in, just motive, opportunity, evidence and witness. And he's got the lot. He had to be that man. And I think he's on the brink of admitting it.'

'You've talked to him again?'

'Like a brother, sir. Just him and me in the sweat-shop. And it's sinking in. There's no exit. Evens that he coughs before court tomorrow.'

I puffed. 'Has he asked to see his wife?'

Tanner shook his head. 'Just the reverse. Says if she

120

comes here we're not to let her in, he doesn't want to see her, now or ever. I'd say he's wise to her. According to Mary, the lady can't wait to see him go down. Is that your impression, sir?'

'My very strong impression.'

'And she was never there when he left the house?'

'No. She was in other company. Just a few streets from here. In Kensington.'

Then I took him over the ground: Eversley Square, Bogey's Bar, Kendal Terrace: gave him the timings, including the six minutes between Kendal Terrace and the hotel. He listened with a comical expression: wanted to interrupt, but didn't. Finally he looked away, then back at me, sideways.

'It can't be on, sir. Can't be! There's too much adding up to chummie.'

'It's on the table. We'll have to follow it up. Just in case there is a connection.'

'But they'd need his car-keys.'

'Yes.'

'Oh lor'! And she'd be the one most likely to have them.'

'Motive, opportunity and witness.'

Tanner gave me a tormented look. I said:

'The brush-off in Bogey's Bar was an ad-lib for my benefit. Both Mrs Welles and Maiden were shoving her husband down my throat.'

'Yes – but!' Tanner's head was shaking. 'Look, they could want him put away, sir. But the other, no, I'm not having it, it smells too much like chummie's tea-leaf.'

'There was opportunity.'

'And that's all, sir, and if the bloke had lived in Plaistow not even that. While every other single thing adds up to chummie, with enough evidence to sink a barge.'

'But it would, wouldn't it?'

'No, sir. No. We'll have to look into it, of course. But

121

Welles is charged and he'll stay charged. It's too late to ring in another chummie now.'

I puffed. 'Let's have him in.'

'Right, sir. Anything you like.'

'And meanwhile we shall need Mrs Brackley's statement.'

Tanner picked up the phone as though he hated it.

Tie-less, lace-less, Welles shuffled in and took the chair placed ready for him. He had shaved now, but somehow it made his face look greyer, wearier. Tanner had yielded the desk chair to me. He sat to one side, hands shoved in pockets. I tried to catch Welles's eye, but he kept his gaze fixed on the desk. I said:

'You're still under warning, Welles. You don't have to answer any questions. But I'm going to repeat three words to you, and I'd like you to tell me what they meant. The words are these: "That could change".'

He didn't look up.

'Did you hear me, Welles?'

'They . . . don't mean anything.'

'I'm told they are your words. Spoken after you made that phone call yesterday.'

'But I never said them.'

'We have a witness.'

'A witness . . . you mean Livvy?'

'Not your wife.'

'Not . . . ?' His puzzled grey eyes at last met mine. 'But no one else was there.'

'No one?'

'No. Just Livvy and me.'

'Think carefully, Welles.'

'But it's the truth! Who else was supposed to be there with us?'

I said: 'I've been talking to the man who discovered

122

your father-in-law's true situation. Who accompanied your wife when she went in search of him. And who returned with her to your house.'

'But she came back alone!'

'Think. I'm told you checked with him about his discovery. That he was present at the discussion that followed. Present when you made your phone call.'

His eyes were wide. 'But all that's nonsense! If someone had been there I would have told you. Livvy, she could have been with anyone. But she brought no one back to the house.'

'Does the name Garry Maiden mean anything to you?'

'Him!'

'I can see it does. It was he who quoted the three words I mentioned, and who thought they had a particular construction.'

'But he wasn't there!'

'He says different. And I'm certain your wife will back him up.'

'Livvy . . .' His mouth hung open. 'And of course, you've been talking to Livvy too.'

'To Mrs Welles and Garry Maiden.'

A spasm went over the grey face.

'Well?'

'I don't know, I don't know! What's the use of my denying anything? I'm done for, I know that, I may as well give up here and now.'

'Then Maiden was present?'

'Does it matter? You'll have me believing these things too. And perhaps it's best. I mean . . . me. Perhaps I was born to finish up like this.'

I said: 'Maiden and your wife are lovers. I don't think that comes as any great surprise. They may be lying. It may be that neither of them would be sorry to see you convicted.'

'I don't care. Do what you want with me.'

'And they may not themselves be entirely innocent.'

He groaned and dug fingers into his thighs. 'I told you before. She had nothing to do with it.'

'Nothing?'

'No. Nothing.'

'With all those billions of pounds at stake?'

'Oh God . . . Livvy, Livvy!'

'For the moment, let's suppose she was in it with you.'

He beat on his thighs. 'Listen. You've got me. Isn't that enough? Aren't I enough to pay for poor Ginny? My life inside to pay for hers?'

'I'm afraid not.'

'But if I did it?'

I leaned across the desk. 'Did you, Welles?'

He shrank from me, his mouth quivering. 'All right, then . . . yes. I did it.'

I said. 'I shall ask you questions. But you are not bound to say any more. Is that understood?'

He nodded, sank back in the chair. He looked very pale.

'Half a mo' – I'll call Mary, sir!'

Tanner would liked to have been rubbing his hands. He'd jumped up like an athlete coming off his blocks, and was half-way to the door when I called him back. I drew him aside.

'Leave it.'

'But for crying out, sir – !'

'I want him to talk. Mary's pencil could stop him dead. And she might be wasting her time anyway.'

'Wasting her time . . . ?' Tanner's stare was agonised.

'I'll take full responsibility.'

'But . . .'

I went back to my chair. Then, an unwilling snail, Tanner moved back to his. I said:

'Listen, Welles. All this time you have been denying that your wife had any involvement. Now I need to know just what happened when she returned to the house yesterday. Did Maiden accompany her, or didn't he?'

He faced me desperately. 'Look, I'm confessing. I did it . . . I killed her. Won't that do?'

'It won't do.'

'But it's all you need to know. If I stand up in court . . . if I swear it?'

I shook my head. 'A full statement. Was Maiden present there, or was he not?'

He stared anguishedly. 'What . . . what is *she* saying?'

'Just tell me.'

'All right then. He was!'

I said: 'So then I can believe him when he tells me that, initially, your anger was directed towards him.'

'Yes. Yes.'

'You offered to strike him.'

'Yes, he was there. Whatever he says.'

'But your wife succeeded in calming you down, advised you of what was the real issue.'

'Yes. The real issue.'

'Let's go from there.'

He stared, swallowed, moistened trembling lips. 'I didn't mean to do . . . what I did. Not at first. I just meant to see Charles, talk him round, try to explain.'

'Murder wasn't in your mind.'

'No! All that . . . came later. I thought if I explained, if I apologised – I mean, I've always got on well with Charles. So I rang him intending just that, and that's all Livvy thought I was going to do.'

'When did Maiden leave?'

'I don't remember! I don't remember very much. I suppose it was after I made that call that I began to think . . . but I can't remember.'

'Didn't she leave with Maiden?'

'Perhaps – no! She must have been there when I left. Ask her, she can tell you. She was somewhere in the house.'

'And you left when?'

'It was after six.'

'I'm told that, in fact, it was some time before.'

'Before or after, does it matter? I was there in time for what happened.'

'So now take me through it.'

He was mauling his thighs. 'On the drive there – I don't know! Something kept putting it in my mind. I knew Bertie's, knew the room number, kept turning it over in my head. It was as though I were someone else, a stranger, not the person I normally was at all – as myself, I could never have dreamt of such a thing! I tell you, it wasn't me driving that car.'

'Carry on.'

'Well . . . I arrived there. Nobody saw me drive in and park. Nothing to stop me. I had only to carry out the programme in my head. I needed a weapon, but I'd thought about that, there was the jack-handle in my boot . . . oh, and the gloves of course. I always carry some in the car.'

'You took these items and locked the car.'

'Yes. I – '

'It didn't bother you that there was a witness?'

'A . . . witness?'

'We have a witness.'

His knuckles were white. 'I don't remember! I was in a state, you understand, like a machine working to a programme. What happened is vague, but I'm doing my best. Was it someone in the street?'

'Just carry on.'

'Well, it didn't stop me. I went on into the hotel. I couldn't have met anyone there, or I'd just have carried on through to the lounge.' He licked his lips again. 'I

126

remember the stairs. Then the corridor, I remember that. And the door . . . her door. The number on it. Number ten.'

'So?'

'Oh God, no! It's all a blank after that.'

'You knocked on the door.'

'It's a blank, I tell you. I've wiped it out, don't remember.'

'Your sister-in-law would have been awake, preparing to go down to the lounge. She would have said "Who's there?", and you would have said "It's me, Freddy".'

'Listen, it's a blank!'

'So she opened the door and said something like "Freddy – how lovely!", then she stood back to let you in, and you closed the door behind you.'

'No – please!'

'You struck her, Welles. She couldn't believe what you were doing. There's a bruise on her wrist. She tried to defend herself. You struck her head again and again.'

'No!'

'The blood flew.'

'It's a blank, I tell you, a blank!'

'She went down. There by the door. And you began pulling out and emptying drawers.'

'God, oh no, oh no!'

'That's how the killing was done, Welles.'

He threw himself down on his knees before the desk and beat on it with clenched fists.

'I didn't do it. I didn't. I didn't!'

'You wish to withdraw your confession?'

'Yes. Yes. I didn't do it. I can't go through with this. I can't!'

'You didn't kill your sister-in-law?'

'No. Never. How can you believe I did a thing like that?'

'In the face of so much evidence?'

127

He gave a strangled moan. 'But I didn't do it!'

'Someone did it.'

'Oh, God help me!' Now it was his forehead he beat on the desk. 'It had to be a thief, an outsider, nobody who knew Ginny could have done that.'

'So we're back to square one.'

'I'm sorry. But there's no way I can go through with it.'

'Back to your house. Was Maiden present?'

Dementedly he shook his head.

'And Mrs Welles was absent when you left?'

He clutched his face. 'Oh please. Please.'

I said: 'Then that's all, for the present.'

Frederick Welles burst into sobs.

I nodded to the sweating Tanner, who jumped up to summon Welles's escort. He was led away. Tanner closed the door quietly, came back to squint at me across the desk.

'So what bloody now?'

'We talk to Maiden,' I said.

'Yeah,' Tanner said, 'we talk to Maiden.' He dropped down on the chair vacated by Welles. 'But I've still got my money on chummie.'

'He's the bookies' choice.'

'And he's my choice. Though this Maiden may have questions to answer. But we'll chase him, oh we'll chase him. If there's the least chance for chummie he's going to have it.'

Which was the right spirit.

'Keep me posted,' I said. 'I had an interrupted lunch-hour.'

Outside, a patrol-car had just pulled up, and I met Mrs Brackley again in reception.

9

I saw the cream BMW when I turned into Lime Walk and
Gabrielle opened the door for me as though she had been
on the watch. She made a face at me and nodded to the
lounge, from which was proceeding the sound of voices.

'She arrived a few minutes ago. It is her father's request
that I admit her.'

'What is she after?'

'Do you need ask?' Gabrielle shaped two contemptuous
kisses.

'Well, it will save me the trouble of a trip to Belgravia.'

'You have some questions for the lady, ha?'

I nodded. 'But, in the meantime, I'm about to expire
with hunger and thirst.'

We went through to the kitchen and I broached a bottle
of Adnam's while Gabrielle filled rolls with cheese and
pickle. We could still hear the wheedling voice of the lady
and Reason's abrupt, sometimes passionate responses. I
ate, drank, filled Gabrielle in. She listened intently, and at
last gave an exclamation.

'So! The game is not yet over, though madame's husband still sits in a cell. Till now I am thinking she may
have driven him to this, but not so, yes? He is her
sacrificial lamb.'

'That has yet to be proved.'

'But yes. I am seeing it all now. And the poor husband

suspects, but even yet is under the spell of this ruthless person. He will stand by her, he will sacrifice himself, allow her to flaunt away with her lover, her inheritance. And now she makes her move – in there, this moment, she ingratiates herself with her foolish father.'

'As I said, there is much to prove.'

'Ha – proof!' Gabrielle's eyes sparkled. 'Then will it not end up as Monsieur Charles is saying? He too shall be at grave risk when there is but my lady left to inherit.'

'There is the third sister.'

'Then she must watch out, I do not think she is a match for madame. One sister has gone, what matters another? And the poor old man must not live too long.'

I shook my head. 'We know nothing for certain.'

'But are you not telling me everything fits?'

'Just that there was opportunity. And meanwhile Welles remains the man with the blood on him.'

'An innocent man!'

I shrugged. 'He may yet face up to a full confession. Tanner didn't charge him on a whim, and before now guilty men have shrunk from an admission.'

'Oh, my friend! Then what are you saying?'

'I'm saying that I need to ask questions of the lady.'

Gabrielle looked sulky. I ate, drank, listened. Now Reason's interjections were less plangent. Pauses were occurring; Olivia Welles' voice was softer, more elegiac.

'My friend,' Gabrielle said. 'Listen to your wife. That woman can use men as though they are hand-tools. Her husband, her lover, it matters not, one or other she makes do this thing. And what will she be wishing, ha? I do not think it is to lose her lover. Oh no. And one or the other, it is she who willed what was to be.'

Next door, a silence. I finished off the Adnam's, rose and went through into the lounge.

* * *

130

'You've hung the charge on him, then!'

Reason was seated on the settee. Olivia Welles sat beside him. She had her arm round her father. Her brown eyes pierced us as we entered but she didn't change her pose. Long, ringed fingers were softly smoothing Reason's dishevelled locks.

'Did he confess?'

I shook my head.

'Dear daddy!' Olivia Welles crooned. 'If Freddy is guilty, well, he's guilty. But you musn't expect his wife to believe it.'

'No more of that, my girl. He killed her, and he must pay.'

'Well, we won't argue. But of course, I stand by him. Would you expect a daughter of yours to do less?'

'No more – if you love me as you say!'

'Then no more, daddy. No more. This gentleman must do what he will about Freddy, and we must give support to one another.'

His hazy eyes stared. 'You haven't behaved very well, Livvy.'

'No daddy.' She hung her head. 'But I'm going to make up for it, just you see. We're together again now, and we'll face this thing together, try not to let it hurt us. Father and daughter. You and me.'

Reason fingered his cheek. 'There are daughters and daughters.'

'Forget her, the peevish bitch!' For an instant Olivia Welles's tone hardened, but quickly the emollient note returned. 'Sue was upset, of course, and you know how unstable she can be. She probably didn't mean it, though. You mustn't let it set you against her.'

'Just keep her out of my sight!'

'I will, daddy, I will. And to make it easy, I want you to come and stay with me till all this is over. I mean, you can't be left alone, even though people are being *so* kind.

You need me, and I need you. So let me show you how much I care.'

'I'm not shifting from my flat.'

'Please, dear daddy.' Olivia Welles stroked the scarred cheek. 'Poor mummy would never have forgiven me if I left you to face this alone.'

'Just don't mention your mother, Livvy.'

'But I must, daddy. "Look after Charles" – I can hear her saying it. And now I can. I can take you home, make up just a little for what has happened.' She fluttered eyes at me. 'I'm sure these good people will tell you it's for the best, that you shouldn't be alone in this trouble. And remember that I need you, too.'

'I stay here.'

'But daddy!'

His eyes looked tired. 'You're doing your best, Livvy. And perhaps I should feel grateful for that. But it won't do. Here's where I lost her. And here is where I'm going to stay.'

'I'll make up for it!'

'You mean well, but no.' He eased her away.

'You can come back often – '

'No.' And he turned his face from her.

Her eyes kindled; flashed first at Gabrielle, then at me. 'And I suppose I have you to thank for this – you, who've been sucking up to him from the start!'

'Madame!' Gabrielle snapped. I held up my hand, said:

'Since you are here, Mrs Welles, perhaps you can help me with a few enquiries.'

'Enquiries? What bloody enquiries?'

'Concerning what happened yesterday evening. As you know, I've been talking to Mr Garry Maiden. Would you care to describe your movements last night?'

* * *

132

'Maiden – that'll be the louse who shopped me!'

It was Reason who suddenly, explosively responded. Jerking round, he turned blazing eyes on the no less savage gaze of Olivia Welles.

'I've been trying to think who the bastard was, who might have got his hands on my personal code, and now it's plain – Reg Maiden's son! I should have spotted him from the start.'

I said: 'You know Maiden?'

'Know him! He learned his trade with us. Then he was poached by Henry Tonks, just as he started to be useful. Oh yes. Young Maiden. Now I can see how it fits together. And who did he come running to when he made his big discovery?'

'Daddy, he's only a friend – '

'Don't waste your talent on me, my girl. I remember him, and I know you, and I can pretty well guess the rest. How much have you promised him?'

'Daddy, how can you!'

'Or are you in this up to your neck? Was it you who worked on Freddy, drove him to his bloody crime?'

'You're mad, daddy!'

'Am I? I doubt if this gentleman will agree.'

'I had no idea of what Freddy had in mind.'

'Then tell the gentleman, not me. Because I notice he's still asking questions.'

Olivia Welles swirled her hair and gave me a look that should have killed. 'I've answered his questions. All his questions. He knows every move I made last night. And I don't see why I should have to go on repeating it when I can't help him any more than I have.'

I said: 'Just clearing up points. In the light of fresh information.'

'Oh yes. That bastard Garry.'

'Who claims to have been present when you conferred with your husband.'

'The swine.'

'But – was it true?'

She gave an impatient snatch of the head. 'I was trying to keep him out of it, wasn't I. But the poor fool had to run to you.'

'Then he was there?'

'What if he was?'

I said: 'It makes him a witness to that conference. To the state of mind of your husband. Perhaps, to indications of his intent.'

She eyed me scornfully. 'Just what did he tell you?'

'He said your husband was much disturbed, that he wanted confirmation of your father's solvency and was considering by what means your father could be ingratiated.'

'So what if he did?'

'Maiden was present during the phone call and remembers a remark your husband made afterwards. When you alluded to Mrs DeWitt as an insuperable obstacle your husband observed "That can change". Do you recall this?'

I heard Reason snatch his breath, and his eyes were steely upon his daughter. Olivia Welles threw her head back and gazed at me with lowered lids.

'Should I recall it?'

'Do you?'

'I think a wife would do well to forget.'

'You tricky bitch!' Reason snarled. 'You heard all right, whatever you say.'

I said: 'Well?'

'I seem to remember something. It may not have been those exact words. Everything was so emotional, wasn't it? Perhaps you'd better rely on your loose-mouthed fool.'

'He said it,' Reason rasped. 'And we know what he meant. He'd have had it in mind when he rang me. Oh God and I agreed, let him set it up, never guessed for a moment what the devil was at.'

134

'It seems a small point,' Olivia Welles said. 'Could have meant something, could have meant nothing. And is that all?'

'Some other things,' I said. 'Like what time your husband left the house?'

'I told you that.'

'You were watching TV. A programme that ended at six p.m.'

'So?'

'The problem seems to be that you must have been watching that programme in Kensington.'

Olivia Welles didn't scream, but something like a scream had exploded in her eyes.

'I was home. I was home at that time.'

I shook my head. 'Not according to witness.'

'But I was. I'd been out for a drive. I've admitted all that already. I wanted to cool off, I went for a spin – heaven knows where, but it could have been Kensington. Only I was back in time for my programme, and before it ended Freddy had left.'

'At five p.m. you were in Kensington.'

'Yes, I could have been. Yes, why not?'

'And you remained there until nearly seven.'

Her hands were like claws. 'I'll mark him,' she said. 'I'll mark him for life.'

'So you were in Kensington?'

'The louse.'

'You were visiting Maiden at his flat?'

'The louse, the louse. But why would he tell you? The bastard must have blown his mind.'

'For nearly two hours you were at his flat?'

'You bitch, you whore!' Reason bawled. 'And that was the way you were paying him, was it – hopping into bed like a common strumpet?'

'I wasn't, daddy – I wasn't!'

'You've just admitted it, you slut.'

'No. I didn't go there for that.' She turned on him magnificently. 'It was you, you who were the reason.'

'Me, pismire!'

'Yes – you. Oh, you don't understand me, do you? But I wanted to know, wanted the proof, that you weren't really broke as you pretended.'

'And I shall believe that?'

'Oh, think the worst. I know I'm dirt beside sainted Ginny. But it's true. It's because of you I went round last night to talk to Garry. And if you'd never deceived us all in the first place, then none of this need ever have happened.'

'I? You blame me?'

'Yes. Yes I do. You shouldn't have done it, daddy. You shouldn't. Perhaps poor mummy dying made you a bit queer, but you're to blame for everything.'

Reason was staring with great eyes. 'I'm not hearing this. I'm not!'

'Oh daddy, I'm sorry. But you shouldn't have blamed me. I don't really mean what I'm saying.'

'So I'm to blame?'

'Daddy, I'm sorry. I shouldn't have let that slip out. Perhaps no one's to blame, really, it just happened. One of those things.'

Reason sat looking stunned, eyes empty, mouth hanging.

I said: 'Then we can agree that you were at Maiden's flat last night?'

She gave her swirl. 'I've done with Garry. You should know that if anyone does. I handed him his cards at Bogey's, and that goes. Garry is out.'

'But – last night?'

She glanced at her father. 'It's perfectly true what I said. For months we'd been hearing that daddy was broke, and that he'd been near to prosecution. Freddy insisted I shouldn't see him, said his own good name would be at stake, and I had to admit the sense of that, however much I longed to see daddy.'

Reason groaned, rocked himself.

'So, you see, I just had to be certain. Oh, I know Freddy went over it all with Garry, but it was shop-talk and half of it I didn't understand. And it was such a shock. If it was true, daddy was richer than ever he was. And that was wonderful. But I had to be certain. So that's why I charged off round to Garry's.'

'For confirmation?'

'Yes.'

'Between five p.m. And say, ten to seven?'

'At least that. And it was five when I got there, because I checked as I was ringing the bell.'

'For those two hours, near enough, you were with Maiden in his flat?'

'Yes.'

'And he with you?'

'Absolutely.'

'Then, if he should tell a different story?'

Her eyes flickered. 'What different story is there to tell?'

'If he should?'

'But he wouldn't, would he. Unless he's a bigger liar than I thought him. What's he saying?'

I kept staring.

'Oh, you slut!' Reason groaned. 'Up there whoring with your toy-boy, while all the time, not far off – '

'Daddy, I wasn't – '

'Don't lie! That's the story your toy-boy tells. You were paying the price, while your devil husband was doing his work down the road.'

'No!'

'Yes!'

Her stare was murderous. Then her lids sank very

137

slightly. 'All right then! Have it if you will. Yes, I was up there screwing Garry.'

'Monster!'

'You foolish old man. Haven't you had your share in your time? And now you're past it, and I'm not. I'm having men from here to breakfast.'

'Bitch, I'll ruin you!'

He'd staggered to his feet, and Olivia Welles had skipped to hers. They stood glaring at each other, Reason panting, on the shake. She threw her hair back: laughed mockingly.

'So what will you do, old man?'

'I'll – I'll – !'

She laughed again. 'Nothing is what the old man will do. You're past it, daddy. Your day is done. You should be thinking of your grave. It's my time now and I mean to have it. That's what Livvy says to you.'

Reason gasped: 'I curse you, curse you!'

'Oh yes. The privilege of old men. But curses break no bones, dear man. And you'd do better to save your breath.'

Perhaps he thought so too, because he dropped back on the settee, sat slumped, panting, staring. Gabrielle ran to him, but he motioned her away, continued panting, staring at nothing. Olivia Welles swung on me.

'So now we've got our cards on the table. Yes, I was at Garry's flat between five and seven, and yes, I wasn't wasting my time. Isn't that what he told you?'

'But – if Maiden is a liar?'

'Then you'll just have to choose between us. So sorry if I lied about seeing Freddy leave, but I was scarcely on oath, was I?'

I said: 'No more than now.'

Olivia Welles stabbed me with a look. 'And precisely what is that supposed to mean, other than a copper's disapproval?'

138

I said: 'We may have a witness.'

'A witness?'

'One who can add something to the story.'

Her eyes were burning. 'There's nothing to add. I screwed Garry, and that's flat.'

'And if we've heard different?'

'You bugger. You're trying it on. And it's a waste of time.'

'Neither you nor he left the flat?'

'No. And screw your bloody witness.' She snatched up her bag. 'I'm off. I came here to do some good for old daddy. So he won't have it, hard luck, I'll leave him to a pair of vultures like you.'

'Just a moment – '

'Get lost.'

I let her sweep by me. We heard the front-door close with a slam, the thud of the car-door, surge of an engine. Reason was sobbing.

'And I'm to blame . . . !'

Tears flowed down the ravaged cheeks. Blindly, he took Gabrielle's hand between his.

'Oh, that a man should ever breed daughters!'

The phone stayed silent, but not the doorbell; ten minutes later came urgent chimes. I opened the door to a youngish man in a powder-blue suit and silver bow-tie.

'Are you Gently? I'm Jason DeWitt. At the bureau they said I'd find Charlie here. You got him?'

'We've got him.'

'Oh hell, what a way to be meeting people!'

I showed him through. Reason's tears had dried and he was nursing three fingers of scotch. He looked up blearily as DeWitt sprang in, then put down the glass and extended his arms.

'Jaz!'

'Charlie-boy!'

They hugged each other in a tight embrace. The tears dried so recently were flowing again, and DeWitt's own well-polished cheeks were not dry.

'Oh Charlie, I just can't believe it. I'm waiting for someone to tell me it isn't so.'

'She's gone, Jaz. Ginny has left us.'

'But how do I believe it? All the way over . . .'

They hugged each other again, DeWitt a sturdy figure in his gay plumage: it included piebald brogues and a waistcoat in candy-stripe. I'd poured another scotch; at a suitable interval I thrust it into his hand. He grabbed it almost impatiently and downed a quick swallow.

'She rang me, you know that? Wanted to tell me the big news. And all I could think of was what a fool I must look, offering jobs to the man behind Allgemein-Zurich. I was short with her, can you beat that? The last time I was ever to hear her voice. And hell . . . it couldn't have been long . . .' He took another fast nip of scotch.

I said: 'Could you put a time to that call?'

'Hell, no! It was after lunch. Be early evening over here, but don't ask me to work it out.'

'A long call?'

'Nope.'

'Anything special about it that you can remember?'

'Just that it knocked me all of a heap, and that I was glad when she cut it short.'

'She did that?'

'Right. A guy had come to her door with a message.'

'A guy . . . ?'

And suddenly he was staring at me, and I at him. I said:

'Tell me just what you remember.'

'But . . . Jesus Christ!' He couldn't even drink.

'You heard his voice?'

'Yuh – I heard it.'

'A man who said he had a message?'

'A man – a bloody man!' Now he did cop down some scotch.

'So?'

'I could hear the bell go, and Ginny didn't cover the phone. She called out "Yes?", and I could hear him saying "A message for you, Mrs DeWitt". She said "Just a moment", then to me "I've got to go now anyway, Jazzy. But I'll ring you again later".' He squeezed his eyes tight. 'But she never did.'

'How clearly did you hear that voice?'

'Oh Jesus. No. No!'

Reason snarled: 'It was Freddy, Jaz. That was how the swine got in.'

'No, I can't think about it!'

'It was him. If she hadn't hung up – '

'Please, Charlie. Please.'

'You can drive the last nail in his coffin.'

'If I think about it, I'll go mad!'

He sank on a chair, stared at his glass, but didn't seem to know what to do with it. For a moment, a gleam of triumph in Reason's deep-set glare. Then he too slumped down on a chair. I said:

'Did you recognise the voice?'

DeWitt didn't seem at once to hear. At last he drank up all that remained in his glass and began shaking his head. 'Nope.'

'You are familiar with Frederick Welles's voice?'

'Yup. He's my brother-in-law, isn't he? And this guy didn't sound like him.' He gulped. 'And Ginny didn't make like she knew him, either.'

'Of course, he'd disguise his voice!' Reason barked. 'But it was him. Couldn't be another.'

'Ginny would have known.'

'It *had* to be him.'

But DeWitt went on shaking his head. 'Maybe this was

141

some other time. Maybe I wasn't hearing the guy who did it. Maybe it really was some bellhop who'd got a message to deliver.'

I said: 'The staff have been questioned.'

'So I don't know! But it wasn't old Fred. Are you all so darned sure that Freddy did it?'

'The case against him is very strong.'

'Well, I can't help it.' He kneaded the glass. 'Jesus, what a godawful mess! I was cut to bits when I lit in here, but now I feel like no tomorrows. Where are they keeping her? Where's Ginny? I got to see her this one last time.'

'You'll see her.'

'And it has to be Freddy?'

'At the moment, the enquiry is far from closed.'

He paused; looked up. 'You mean – ?'

'Just that the enquiry is continuing.'

I fed him more scotch. Reason seemed to have drifted back into one of his vacancies. DeWitt sat frowning at his refilled glass, but made no attempt to sample it. Finally he looked me in the eyes.

'See here, I thought I knew old Freddy! We both liked him, me and Ginny, and I don't get it that he would do this. He's a softy guy, and straight. There has to be a mistake here. Unless you can produce ten guys who saw him, I'll never believe that Freddy killed her.'

'Of course, you know his wife, Olivia Welles.'

'Don't talk to me about Olivia! That cat slapped my face once, and I was near to spanking her elegant arse. You're telling me she fits in someplace?'

'Would it surprise you if she did?'

His head shook slowly. 'No, sir. No. Not the least bit would it surprise me.' He looked at his glass, at me. 'She was knives into Ginny,' he said. 'Maybe you should be digging around that dame. Maybe you already have.'

'Maybe.'

'Then you'll know. I can't say more in front of Charlie.'

142

'And the voice was a strange voice.'

'Just a limey voice. On the other side of a hotel door.'

'One you'd remember?'

'I'd like to say yes, but so help me one limey voice sounds like another.'

'Thank you, Mr DeWitt.'

'Jaz. I guess you're a regular scout, Gently.'

The phone went; Tanner. Maiden had been located. I drew Gabrielle into the hall and kissed her, among other things.

'Look after the invalids.'

'Aha. Is this then a lead to that frightful woman?'

'We'll see.'

I took the car this time, hoping to be there when Maiden arrived.

10

I was too late. While I was hunting for a slot I saw Maiden being decanted from a patrol-car, and he had been hustled through reception by the time I arrived there. Once more I was assailed by Mrs Strickland.

'Was it him – did he do it?'

'Please, Mrs Strickland!'

'But you've arrested him!'

'Mr Maiden is here to help our enquiries.'

'And that's the same thing – you've got him. And now will you be letting Freddy go?'

'We are pursuing our enquiries.'

'You bastard! You've known Freddy was innocent all along – '

I signalled to the prowling Mary, and hastened through to Tanner's office.

Tanner had both DI Pyatt and DS Edith with him, and Maiden had just been allotted the hot seat. Somewhat reluctantly, Tanner rose and made way for me at the desk. If the array of talent appeared formidable it was seeming to have little effect on Maiden, who had risen when I entered, and now faced me with an amused smile.

'You didn't have your drink, but don't worry – it wasn't wasted!'

Hands in pockets, legs sprawled, he couldn't have presented a more casual attitude. Tanner was staring at him bleakly, with Pyatt and Edith giving their support. But it was all lost on Maiden, who might have been relaxing with mates at Bogey's. I said:

'You know why you're here, Maiden.'

'Of course. You want a statement from me, all that.'

'Before you make it I have some questions to put to you.'

'Which naturally I shall do my best to answer. But remember this.' His eyes were steady. 'You're talking to a pal of old Freddy's. I've said what I said and I'll stand by it. But further than that I may not be helpful.'

'I will bear it in mind.'

'No offence intended. But you must allow for my situation. I'm in somebody's bad books now, and I should hate to get in any deeper. Understood?'

'I think I understand.'

It got me a blue smile. 'So fire away. I'll be only too pleased to dot the i's, cross the t's.'

'Just a routine point first,' I said. 'You tell me you were present at the Welles house yesterday. Mrs Welles seems uncertain of that, and her husband doesn't remember it at all.'

The blue eyes never faltered. 'Oh!'

'Can you throw any light on that?'

'If they don't want to remember, that's understandable. It doesn't do Freddy's cause much good.'

'Then both of them are lying?'

'Let's say forgetful. You can't expect miracles of human nature.'

'And you were there?'

He rocked his shoulders. 'Unless their two words are better than my one.'

I nodded. 'And you left when?'

'Soon after Freddy made his call.'

'To go where?'

'Back to my pad. I felt I could use a little peace.'

145

'And there you remained?'

'Right there. I can't assist you after that. I knew nothing more of the matter until a phone call from Livvy this morning.'

I said: 'Can that be vouched for?'

'Livvy will tell you she made the call.'

I said: 'Not the phone call.'

His smile was a little sideways. 'Not the phone call.'

'Well?'

'Let me guess. You've made the acquaintance of our Mrs Brackley.'

'And?'

'Did she mention a lady?'

I said: 'We have certain information.'

'Yes,' Maiden smiled. 'Now I'm with you. Did you know that Lolly was a Tiller Girl?'

'Do you mind if I smoke?'

From a pocket in the baggy blouson he produced a cigar. It fetched a dirty look from Tanner, but Maiden lit it just the same. It smelled expensive. Maiden leaned back, exhaled smoke smoothly towards the ceiling. It suggested a TV advert, and perhaps that was how he was seeing it. He cocked a look at me.

'You know, I'd rather sooner not tell tales! I mean even in these enlightened times some of us draw a line somewhere. And it won't help you. A naughty bachelor spending one of his naughty evenings. So what? Even if Lolly could name the lady, which I gravely doubt.'

'I have spoken to that lady.'

'Oh. I see.' He took a considered puff. 'So there's not much use in my being gallant. Supposing you had any doubt in the first place.'

'How long was she with you?'

'Well . . . long enough!'

146

'Perhaps you can be more specific.'

'If I must. Say a couple of hours. But really my mind wasn't on the clock.'

'Beginning when?'

'Oh dear! I'd say she followed me over here. I got back a few minutes before five, and she was on my doorstep not long after that.'

'And she left when?'

'Seven, about. She was bothered that Freddy wouldn't find her in. He might have got a rough reception at Bertie's and gone home before he was expected.'

'And that would have bothered her?'

'But yes. She was supposed to be waiting, agog for his news. She'd told him she was going out to visit Sue, her other sister, and would try to be back before he left. Of course she wasn't, but seven was the latest she dared hang about with me.'

'So she was with you for those two hours?'

'Cut my throat if I tell a lie.'

'And you were with her?'

'I'm afraid so.'

'For each and every minute of that time?'

'Doesn't she say so?'

'I'm asking you.'

He shook his head. 'I go along with the lady! If she has a tale to tell more innocent, then I'd better not give her the lie. So what does she say?'

I said: 'Let me repeat. We have certain information.'

Maiden smiled, but not quite at me. The cigar remained smoking in his hand. He glanced winningly at the stone-faced Tanner, the earnest Pyatt, the humourless Edith. Finally he leaned forward to, very deliberately, tap ash from the cigar into Tanner's ashtray. He sighed.

'Ah me! I can see I shall have to come clean, shan't I? After all, I had the boot from the lady, and it's up to her if she fibs to you blokes. It won't help you, of course, but

147

never mind. You have to get these things straight. And with Lolly twitching her curtain I never had a chance in the first place, did I?' He puffed firmly. 'Right, then. So it wasn't a sex session up there. Sex was the last thing in the lady's mind when she bowled up and rang my bell.'

'Go on.'

'Livvy was livid. With her husband, her father and, for some reason, me. We were all in a tale, it seemed, to do her down and despite her. Her dad had deceived her, Freddy was useless, and me, I'd left it too late. If I had warned her a few days earlier she might have put skids under young Ginny. No good my excusing myself, it only added fuel. You've seen yourself what she can be like, and – ' he chuckled – 'she was being like herself.'

'So.'

'Well, I wanted to get rid of her! I'd had quite enough of Livvy for one fine day. So at last I said sorry and all that, but I've an errand to run, I shall have to go out.'

'And did that get rid of her?'

'If only it had. But Livvy saw through my little game. She said she'd wait till I got back, and I'd better be quick if I valued our friendship.'

'And that was when?'

'What does Lolly say?'

I stared into the smiling eyes.

'Oh well, say sixish. Thereabouts. But the time was the last thing on my mind.'

'You left Kendal Terrace at six p.m.?'

'If we're being formal, yes.'

'And proceeded in which direction?'

'Towards the park . . . eventually.'

'Eventually?'

The smile never wavered. 'I'd told her I had to see a bookie in Church Street. So I set off that way, in case she was watching, then doubled back towards the park.'

'At six p.m. you were going towards Church Street.'

148

'Yes, but only to the end of Kendal Terrace.'

'You were within six minutes' walk of Church Street?'

'Five. If you happen to be in a hurry.'

I let it lie. Tanner and his crew were almost holding their breaths. Maiden smiled on. He had a dimple in his chin, and no seaming at all in the smooth, tanned cheeks. In another room, a typewriter was clicking perhaps making a copy of Mrs Brackley's statement. I said:

'You went towards the park?'

'Right. As far as the gate to Holland House.'

'That wouldn't have taken long.'

'Five minutes at the most. And I was in no hurry to be getting back.'

'So?'

'So I lit a cigar, hung around, strolled up and down. Watched some hostellers going in. And some others coming out. It was dull work, but I was hoping she would take the hint and go. I suppose I killed half an hour. But when I got back, there she was.'

'Between six and six-thirty you were smoking a cigar near Holland House.'

'Absolutely.'

'Can you prove that?'

'Off the cuff, no I can't. Does it matter?'

'I think it matters.'

Still he smiled. 'I can't think why. Of course, someone may have seen me, or you could look for the stub of my cigar. But proof or not that's where I was. Between six p.m. and six-thirty.'

'Then a witness who saw you elsewhere is mistaken.'

'Oh quite. Was there one?'

'Who places you much nearer to Church Street. As near as the car-park of Bertie's Hotel.'

'Oh dear me.' He smiled at the cigar. 'Yes, I can see what you're getting at now. There am I, loose in Kensington, just when everything is going on. The right time, and

149

if only I had been in the right place. Too bad I wasn't. But that's life. I can't help you there at all.'

'Yet if you were seen there?'

'I wasn't. Put it down to a trick of the light. Going and coming, nowhere near. Take it that's the definitive statement.'

'And – Mrs Welles?'

'What about her?'

'For half an hour, she was left on her own. Five minutes, by your reckoning, from Bertie's. Between the times of six p.m. and six-thirty.'

And for once he didn't smile. 'Are you being serious?'

I didn't reply, kept staring.

'But – that's ridiculous! She was at the flat. Both when I left and when I got back.'

'But in between?'

'You can't seriously think – '

'Once more, we have certain information.'

Now the smile had definitely gone into storage. And the cigar had acquired a dither. He stared at me, at the stony Tanner: almost with pleading in his gaze.

'Look, I know she never left the flat. Anything else and she would have told me. She said she would wait for me and she did. She was sitting with a drink when I got back there.'

'The hotel was close. She could not but be curious.'

'But she didn't go there. She wouldn't.'

'Why wouldn't she?'

'Because! It would be too stupid, the way things were.'

'How were they, Mr Maiden?'

'Well, it's obvious. Her turning up there would have made matters worse. It was all up to Freddy, wasn't it, and she had to give him a free field.'

'To do what?'

'To do – ?' And I'd never seen the blue eyes larger. But then they slowly, teasingly relaxed, began to shape again

150

for the smile. 'Lay off it! You're stringing me along. This famous information of yours is a dud. Of course Livvy never left the flat. If she had, it would have been to chase after me.'

I said: 'Listen, Mr Maiden. For that half hour she doesn't have an alibi, and neither do you. Five minutes away a woman was murdered who stood in her way, and perhaps in yours. Her husband may also have been an obstacle. He sits here in a cell, charged with that murder. And she has lied to us and you have lied to us. And the matter will not rest here.'

His smile embraced the company. 'I love it,' he said. 'No stone unturned. I should have been a policeman. This really gets to me. You look at it every which way. But you're up a blind alley here. Livvy didn't shift and I wasn't there. If Freddy didn't do it, blood and all, then you'll have to look somewhere else for a candidate.'

I said: 'Blood and all?'

'So wasn't there blood on his car?'

'Was there, Mr Maiden?'

'You know there was.'

I said: 'But I'm wondering how you know.'

The smile was on ice. 'Livvy told me.'

'Then I'm having to wonder how Mrs Welles knew.'

'Say her father told her.'

'But Mr Reason had no opportunity to inspect the car.'

'Well then – she made a good guess! Or it may have been me who did the guessing. It's obvious, isn't it? You've got some strong evidence. And there was blood on his sleeve. The old man saw it.'

'But – on the car?'

'All right – not the car! You know, and I'm only guessing.'

'But such a confident guess?'

'Leave it out. All I meant was you'd got the goods on Freddy.' The smile eased back, took in Tanner for a

151

moment. 'But don't think I'm not appreciating all this! You're doing your best to play it square with Freddy. It just happens you're up the wrong tree. So I'm the nuisance who started all this, you have to put me through the mill. But honestly, what have you got? Just that I was in Kensington without an alibi. That won't stand up, will it? So a good try, chaps. And thanks for the party.' He ground out the cigar. 'And now, if I may, I'll make that statement and stop wasting your time.'

Tanner looked at me: I nodded. Tanner nodded to Edith.

'If you'll come this way, sir,' Edith said.

Maiden rose, beamed and followed Edith out.

The door closed; Tanner stared at it, then cracked the knuckles of his large hands. He said: 'I'd love to. Oh, I'd love to. But sir, that grinning ape is right.'

'It won't stand up.'

'No sir. Though I'd swear he's in it up to his chin. Him and her both. But Welles is the chummie who did it.'

'They set him on.'

'Right.'

'You think he could have been such a tool?'

'Yes sir. The lady owns him. Even now he's trying to keep her out of it.'

'Even knowing about Maiden?'

'Even that. He'll go on taking it on the chin. He belongs to her, body and soul. And we bloody know it. But that's all.'

I shook my head. 'We just talked to chummie.'

Tanner looked at me sidelong, then shook his head too. 'I can't go along with that, sir. Much as I'd love to put him inside.'

I said: 'Olivia Welles should have been his alibi. Too bad they couldn't make it stick. But that's what was intended. And now it's bust. All we need is one scrap of evidence.'

Still Tanner's head wagged. 'Need more than a scrap, sir! With all we've got stacked against Welles. Then there's the little matter of credibility. I'm trying, but it sticks in my throat.'

I said: 'Maiden was loose at just that time. Five minutes, he says, in either direction. He'd be concealed there when Welles arrived and he was provided with the keys of Welles's car.'

'Yes, it's possible, sir, but – '

'He unlocks the car, takes the jack-handle, enters the hotel, ascends the back stairs, makes his way to the bedroom the number of which he knows. There he rings the bell and calls through the door that he has a message for Mrs DeWitt.'

'But that's guess-work, sir – '

'No. We have a witness that that's what happened.'

'A – witness?'

'Hot from New York. She was phoning her husband when the killer arrived.'

I told him about Jason DeWitt; Tanner listened with doubtful eyes. He said:

'But it could as well have been Welles at the door, sir. Don't see how you can tie that to Maiden.'

'It wasn't Welles. The voice was one that neither DeWitt nor his wife recognised. And Welles wouldn't have needed to play games. His sister-in-law would have opened the door to him.'

'Perhaps one of the staff we haven't questioned – '

'That's a coincidence too many! It was the killer waiting outside that door, which she went to open after she'd hung up. So she died, and the killer ransacked the room, and probably soaked those gloves in her blood. Then he grabbed her bag, wrenched the brooch off her, went back

153

down the stairs and to Welles's car. Ten minutes I think we said?'

'Well . . . yes.'

'And five minutes more back to the flat. The lady gets his report, then hurries home to be found there when the news breaks.'

'It is possible, sir, but . . .'

'All we need is that one piece of evidence.'

But Tanner went on shaking his head, and I wasn't getting much reaction from Pyatt, either. I said:

'Can we get a quick search-warrant?'

'Might take time, sir. On a Sunday. And we'd have to persuade the beak that we'd got something solid to go on.'

'We need to turn that flat over.'

'Yes sir. I can see how you're thinking.'

'One spot of blood on his clothes would outweigh all we have against Welles.'

'Yes sir. But would we find it, if chummie is as clever as you think? More like any evidence of that sort would be floating down the Thames.' He cracked his knuckles again. 'I don't like him any better than you do, sir. But for all we've got against him he can still walk free through that door.'

I said: 'Call him back in here.'

'Sir?'

'At least, he can turn out his pockets.'

Tanner didn't look thrilled, but he did as I said. Maiden wasn't smiling when he came back in. But that changed when I curtly requested him to empty his pockets on the desk. Then he smiled.

'I thought you wouldn't ask me!'

'Have you any objection?'

'None.'

He began laying out wallet, change, cigars, lighter and a set of car-keys with a Porsche tag.

'That's the lot.'

'Feel him over.'

Pyatt hastened to perform the chore.

'Now turn around slowly under the light.'

His sugar-bag clothes were spotless.

'Is that it?'

'For the moment.'

'Then I'll go back and finish my little task.'

Grinning, he collected his possessions and redistributed them about his person. At the door he turned to give me a final beam, but then had to make way for the sergeant from reception. The latter closed the door behind Maiden. He said:

'Sir, there's an American bloke out front. Says he's the husband of the victim, and demands to see the prisoner.'

'Well he can't!' Tanner snapped.

'That's what I've been trying to tell him, sir. But he's going on about her having been an American citizen, and how he'll call in the embassy if we don't play ball.'

'Tell him he can call in Ronald Reagan if he likes.'

'Hold it!' I said. 'What else does he say?'

'Says we've got the wrong man, sir, and he's damn sure the prisoner knows who did it.'

'Yeah,' Tanner said. 'He's a clever boy. But tell him there's rules and we don't break them.'

'Wait,' I said. 'Ask him to step in here. And have the prisoner Welles standing by.'

Tanner's eyes were popping. 'You can't, sir!'

'I will take full responsibility.'

'But it's breaking every bloody rule!'

'The rules weren't written for this situation.'

'But . . . bloody hell!'

The sergeant left. Moments later, DeWitt bounced in. He said:

'Listen, Gently, Charlie's been giving me the dirt. And

155

there's no damned doubt who killed Ginny, it's a lover-boy creep called Maiden. It's as plain as my arse, so why are you still holding poor old Freddy? He's only covering for his goddamn wife. And I'll bet you know that as well as me.'

I said: 'Take a seat, Mr DeWitt.'

'Oh sure – but do I get to see Freddy?'

'If you can promise me you're not carrying a gun.'

Jason DeWitt said something naughty.

Pyatt fetched Welles in, and for a moment he didn't notice DeWitt seated by the window. When he did, he started back apace, almost shedding a laceless shoe.

'Jaz . . . no.'

'It's all right, Freddy-boy!'

DeWitt sprang up, spread his hands towards Welles.

'Jaz . . . I didn't.'

'No, you goddamn didn't. And I never for one moment thought you did.'

'But I've been charged . . .'

'They framed you, Freddy-boy. You've been framed from here to Minnesota.'

'Charlie thinks . . .'

'Not now, Freddy-boy. I've talked the old buzzard out of that.'

'But . . .'

Welles stood rocking, eyes staring, mouth gaped. Then DeWitt moved across to him, embraced him, hugged him the way he'd hugged Reason.

'It's all right, you lug – it's all right! We'll get you out of here don't you worry. Because we know who did do it, huh? And we've got Charlie pitching for us too.'

'But . . .'

'Hell, there aren't any buts! Just you speak up, tell them

156

all you know. I guess they're half-way there already, and maybe you can give them the dope to clinch it.'

'No . . .'

'Go man – go!'

'I can't Jaz.'

'Blow his tits off!'

'No!'

'Listen, that creep killed Ginny, you going to let him get away with that?'

Welles pushed DeWitt away from him. 'I can't help it! You don't understand – '

'Oh yes I do, Freddy. And hell, she isn't worth it. And you've got to face that, you've just got to.'

'I don't know anything – '

'Listen, it was lover-boy. And lover-boy had to have information. And where's he getting it from, huh? Who can tell him where and when?'

'I don't believe it!'

'You believe it, Freddy. And another thing. That junk in your car. He had to have the keys for that, pardner, and you tell me where else he could get those.'

'I may have left it unlocked – '

'And pigs can fly. She set you up, brother. No other way. And the cops know it, they have to know it.' He spun on me. 'You going to tell me different?'

I said: 'The investigation will continue.'

'Never mind the crap, are you getting after him?'

'Now you listen to me, sonny-boy!' Tanner rapped. 'I've heard enough of this comic stuff from you. Maybe that's the way it is in the States, but it gets you nowhere over here. We do things our way, and let me tell you that a charge has been made, and that charge stands. We know about Maiden. We've talked to Maiden. And so far there's nothing that ties him in. You with me?'

'But it's goddamn obvious – '

'I'll decide what's obvious, sonny-boy! And we've bent

157

the rules far enough just letting you have this chat with the prisoner.'

'For gosh-sakes, I'd never have believed – '

Came a tap on the door; a patrolman entered. He said:

'Sorry to interrupt, sir, but I thought you should know about these. We found them shoved down in the seat of the car we used to pick up Garry Maiden.'

And he laid a bunch of car-keys on the desk, a bunch with a tag that showed a Viking ship.

I said: 'Are these yours, Welles?'

He was staring at them as though at a ghost. DeWitt grabbed his arm and shook him – 'Tell him, Freddy – oh hell, tell him!'

Welles held out a trembling hand. I placed the bunch of keys in it. Welles stared at them, his face working, then slammed them suddenly down on the desk. He grasped DeWitt and hung on to him, sobbing.

'They are – they sure as hell are!'

Tanner came off his chair with a snarl. 'That grinning bastard – just let me get at him!' He shoved past Welles and DeWitt and flung open the door. 'Fetch Maiden in here!'

A moment later a sheepish Edith appeared, a sheet of statement-paper in his hand.

'Maiden's gone, sir. Ten minutes ago. But I got his statement down all right.'

'You mean you let him leave?'

'Yes sir . . . he gave me one of his cigars.'

Tanner's face rose in mute supplication. Then he hurled himself on the phone.

158

11

'His car has gone. The bastard has scarpered.'

That was the news from Kendal Terrace, regularly confirmed by Mrs Brackley, with the addition that Maiden had arrived and departed in a tearing hurry. Meanwhile the tearful Welles, supported by his brother-in-law, had been put in storage in an interview room, where the WPC, Mary, was plying both of them with mugs of strong tea. And I had been on the phone to Gabrielle, to pass on cautious news to Reason.

'Well he won't get far in that bloody Porsche. It stands out like a monkey's arse.'

I shrugged. 'He knows now that we're on to him. Soon that car is going under cover.'

'The cunning sod. And he was on the premises not more than twenty minutes ago. And me still sucking in his mallarkey – Gordon Bennett, what a mug!'

I said: 'As yet, he can't be certain that those keys have turned up.'

Tanner's eyes were small. 'You mean – ?'

'What would your next move have been?'

Tanner kept staring. 'Christ, yes!' His hand went to the phone, but I stopped him.

'My car is unmarked. And we need a word with the lady too.'

'So let's get over there, sir!'

'Just warn the cars in the area.'

Tanner did, and then we went, brushing aside Susan Strickland in reception. Traffic was easy and we made good time to Eversley Square. I drove round it.

'No bloody Porsche!'

Perhaps that was not to be expected. The cream BMW was parked out front and I slid into a slot close by. We went up the steps and rang. There was light behind curtains in the lounge and in the hall. I rang again. Still we had to wait before the door was cautiously opened.

'You!'

She tried to slam the door, but my foot was planted in it.

'I'm afraid you must admit us, Mrs Welles.'

'You pig. I refuse, do you hear?'

'I think you must realise the situation.'

'I realise nothing – take your foot from my door!'

'Both your friend and yourself are under grave suspicion.'

'Just take yourelf and your suspicions elsewhere!'

'I regret this.'

I pushed on the door, and she was forced to back into the hall. She stood glaring, panting, tossing her hair, looking as though at any moment she meant to attack me.

'You bastard, forcing your way in here! Couldn't you at least have rung me first? After that little session this afternoon I should have thought you could have left me in peace. What's your game?'

I said: 'We have talked to Maiden.'

'Garry! Well, you know what I think of him. If you want to run him in, good luck to you. But don't expect any help from me.'

I said: 'Where is he?'

'Where? Don't you know? And you really think you will find him here?' She laughed mockingly. 'That's rich. And you're supposed to be one of the bright ones.'

'May we come in?'

'Please do. Who am I to stand in you bastards' light? And I was only watching some lousy television, so do come in and make yourselves at home.'

And in fact we could hear the television proceeding from the trendy lounge, towards which she retreated. Tanner whispered:

'Perhaps he's still on his way, sir.'

'Take a stand by the window and watch the square.'

We entered the lounge; Tanner, as bid, went to the window and twitched a curtain aside. I switched off the television.

'Now. In case there is any misunderstanding. You are under suspicion of conspiring with Garry Maiden in the murder of your sister, Mrs DeWitt.'

She swung her hair. 'You dear man. Next, tell me a story from the Brothers Grimm. And get it into your crooked little mind that he was screwing me when Ginny was bonked.'

'No, Mrs Welles.'

'Oh but yes. I could give you a blow by blow account. He may be a tale-bearing stinker, but he can handle himself when it matters. I arrived at five, yes? And we didn't waste time in the prelims. Then it was hammer and tongs, little man, until I had to be getting back here. Immoral of course. But true. We were banging from five till a quarter to seven.'

I said: 'I have different information.'

'You mean, that we stopped for a drink at half-time?'

'That Maiden was absent from the flat. At the critical time when your sister was killed.'

'Oh lovely. A man about a dog. But now you're hearing the facts from me.'

I said: 'Information confirmed by Maiden.'

'Oh la! I forgot you'd been talking to him.'

'So?'

161

'You bloody fool. What do you think the wimp would say?' She tossed her hair mightily. 'A tale about running an errand, was it? How I was giving him a hard time, and how he went out, hoping I would blow? Something like that! He was going to tell it if my precious honour was at stake. And you shook it out of him, you sweetie, and you'd love to believe it was true.'

'And you know he told me that?'

'Of course. It was the fib he had all ready.'

'No, Mrs Welles. It was a lie he improvised. About which you could know in only one way.'

'Because he told me. At the flat.'

'Because he was here. A very short time ago. When he told you that the game was up and that he must conceal himself from the law.'

Her laugh was icy. 'Isn't that likely? That Garry tell-tale would show up here? You're out of your mind, little man – or is it that daddy is pulling the strings?'

'Where is Garry Maiden, Mrs Welles?'

'Go and look for him, you sod.'

'You might do well to be more co-operative.'

'Go to hell! And take him with you.'

At which point Tanner gave an exclamation: and I had heard the sound too. Not at the front of the house, but the back: the squeak of a sash-window being stealthily opened.

'Come on, sir!'

Tanner had dropped his curtain in a flash. We charged out of the lounge and down the hall to the room from which the sound had come.

'Chummie's bolted the door!'

Tanner crashed his lanky frame against it. It resisted: two more attempts were needed before the bolt yielded and we plunged through. We had entered a dining-room, with a long table and chairs that got in the way, and, at the further end, an open window and fluttering curtain.

162

We raced to it. Outside, a small garden, bounded by a wall with a door that hung open. Tanner, swearing, was just about to vault through the window when we heard the clunk of a car door and the growl of an engine.

'Back to the car – those mews are a cul-de-sac!'

We galloped back through the house. Olivia Welles screamed after us: 'I hope you kill yourselves, you bastards!' And we were too late. I was still fumbling for the ignition when the red Porsche emerged in the square, turned sharply and rocketed away, heading east on a route that the driver would know well.

'Go on – kill yourselves – kill yourselves!'

Her screams died in the roar of the engine. Tanner was already at the radio. I sent the Rover squealing after the red car. Traffic baulked us, baulked the Porsche. It took a chance and squirmed through. Then a break let me in and I was on his tail, though well back.

'The sod, he was there all the time – listening to us, like as not!'

'So now he knows the chips are down.'

'The boys will get the bastard if we don't.'

It looked as though we wouldn't, and that even the boys would have their hands full. A patrol car that tried to break in from a junction was passed both by the red car and by us. Sirens sounded behind, but ahead our quarry was pulling out a lead, taking chances, sprinting for gaps, putting ever more vehicles between us and him.

'Where do you think he's heading, sir?'

'Just east.'

'It'll be a rum old job if we lose him.'

Yes it would. And he wasn't short of means. It was a well-stuffed wallet he'd laid on the desk. But now the traffic was congealing, and even the Porsche was being closed down and held in line. Nose to tail the queues ambled, solid lanes in either direction. Behind, the frustrated sirens. Ahead, lights, showing a tantalising green.

Then amber. Then red. Then amber and once more green. And the gap occurred, the slimmest gap, between the queues coming and going: and into that gap leaped the Porsche, followed in a moment by ourselves. But he was leaving us handsomely, going like a bullet for the lights, lights that had almost spent their green, lights that were amber, lights that were red. And suddenly, like a dream, the Porsche rushed back towards us with its tyres gushing smoke, and slowly, so slowly, crossed ahead of it the towering bulk of a container-truck. Slowly. It all happened slowly. As though the camera had glue in its works. The smoking Porsche, the creeping truck. And the one submarining under the other.

'Bloody . . . hell!'

And I braked just in time, as the gap closed in ahead of us. Tanner had his door open, I mine, and we dodged round the vehicles to the crumpled Porsche. But the truck-driver had got there first. He was staring at the wreckage with popping eyes. Tanner caught him as he reeled away. He gurgled:

'Oh God – it's taken his bloody head off!'

I looked. And it had. And now the uniform-men came running.

'Get back – get back – it could go up!'

Which in fact was what happened a few seconds later.

It took an hour to disperse the traffic and free the Rover from the jam that built up, and by then the wreck was covered with foam and firemen were setting up lifting gear. The body had gone: most of it; and they'd taken the truck-driver away too. Tanner looked as though he might have wished to join him, his face grey and tight. In the car, he said:

'We'll have to have the lady, sir.'

'First we'll let Welles off the hook.'

'Yes sir. But we'll have to have her. And that's something I'm not looking forward to.'

Neither was I, and I broke no records in tooling the Rover back to Kensington. I could imagine scenes that I would rather have avoided when we came to arrest Olivia Welles.

Reason's Mini was parked at the police station and he was waiting for me inside. He began:

'Look, what Jaz was saying has bothered me, and according to Suzy-Lu – '

'Just hold it for a moment.'

I went through with Tanner. Pyatt was manning the office phone. He said:

'We've just heard what happened, sir. One of our cars was at the scene and brought the news.'

I said: 'Now I've a job for you. You're to take a car to Eversley Square. Have Mary and one of her mates with you. You're to arrest Mrs Welles and bring her back here.'

'Arrest her, sir?'

'She may give trouble, in which case you are authorised to use the cuffs. Also, when you return here, you'll bring her in the back way and not through reception.'

Pyatt swallowed. 'Is that all, sir?'

'And make sure that Mary's mate has some muscle.'

Pyatt bowed himself out. Tanner said:

'Thanks, sir. I wasn't feeling up to that job myself.'

I said: 'Now we come to the family. Better ask them to step in here.'

'They came. First, Reason and his daughter, then Welles, with DeWitt following behind. Reason, who had been shown to a chair, jumped up again when his son-in-law entered. Welles hung back. They stood staring at each other, two dogs, each suspecting the other's intention.

165

Finally Reason sat down again, his eyes still fastened on the shrinking Welles. He snapped:

'What is he doing here?'

DeWitt placed his hand on Welles's arm. 'Lay off him, Charlie-boy,' he said. 'It's over. Freddy never did it.'

'And I'm saying he did!'

'You're up the creek, man. The cops and all know he was framed.'

'That's your tale, Jaz, but I'm not buying it. I saw him with fresh blood on his sleeve.'

DeWitt said: 'So ask the cops, man. They're out hunting that sonofabitch Maiden now.' He turned to me. 'You tell him, Gently. Tell him it was lover-boy who killed my wife. And hear me right. If I get to arm's-length of him I'll have the black heart out of his body.'

I said: 'Garry Maiden is dead.'

'What's that?'

'He's dead. He was killed in a car crash.'

'You're telling me – ?'

'Garry Maiden is dead. And we have sent to arrest his accomplice.'

DeWitt was staring. 'This isn't a con?'

'We discovered him at the house in Eversley Square. He escaped in his car. A chase followed, and he died in an accident with crossing traffic.'

'For crying out!' DeWitt exclaimed. 'And you've gone to pick up Livvy?'

'I regret that is unavoidable. On the evidence she will have to be charged.'

'I'll say she will!'

'Oh no!' The agonised cry came from Welles. 'You can't do that – Livvy isn't responsible. And if the man who killed Ginny is already dead – '

'Freddy-boy, get wise!'

'He used Livvy, and now he's dead.'

'She set you up, Freddy. She wanted the dough, wanted to clear you out of her way.'

'No, it's too heartless! He's dead. Please God, let it end there. I don't care what evidence you've got, she isn't responsible. She was used.'

'Oh Freddy, wake up!'

'You don't know her, Jaz. Please, let her go free!'

'Silence, you puppies!' Reason had slowly risen from his chair once more. He came to the desk, confronted me, peered at me with hooded eyes. 'Is this true?'

'It's true.'

'My son-in-law was framed?'

'He was framed.'

'No question?'

'No question.'

'Maiden killed her?'

'Yes.'

He stood wavering an instant at the desk, his eyes cast down, then turned slowly about to face his anguished son-in-law. He said:

'Sorry, Frederick.'

'Oh Charles!'

'I should have known you better.'

'Charles . . .'

Reason opened his arms, took his son-in-law in his embrace. Over his shoulder, he said to me:

'And you're dropping all charges?'

'All charges are dropped.'

'He's free.'

'He is free.'

'Oh, I never doubted it – never!' Susan Strickland was on her feet now. She grabbed her brother-in-law's arm and tenderly clung to him.

'Off, you bitch!' Reason snarled. 'All your love is in your claws.'

'But I knew – I knew all along. When you were swearing he should be hung.'

167

'Off, off!'

'I knew, Freddy. When daddy and all the world were against you. When the stupid police charged you. Still I knew you could never have done it.'

Welles looked embarrassed. 'It was good of you, Suzy – '

'Yes, I never doubted for a moment! I told them. It wasn't in you. You were gentle, you were kind.'

'I'll remember – '

'Oh Freddy, and it's over – over in more ways than one. You're free now, a free man. And perhaps it wasn't such a bad thing after all.'

'Get your hands off him!' Reason snarled. 'We know your game, Suzy-Lu. You're no better than the she-wolf your sister. You'd play the same pranks tomorrow.'

'Daddy, that's a terrible thing to say!'

'Oh yes, my lady, you're no better. She killed a sister, and so would you if it fitted in with your little schemes.'

'Now, now, Charlie-boy,' DeWitt chided. 'This thing has got us all knocked-up. But it's no good blaming Suzy-Lu, we've got to hang in here together.'

Reason quelled him with a look; then he turned to me again.

'That bitch. You've got her fixed – no chance of some clever-dick getting her off?'

I said: 'Mrs Welles provided the car-keys and the number of your daughter Virginia's room. She was present at Maiden's flat in Kensington before, during and after the commission of the crime. They concerted a lie to strengthen suspicion against her husband, and she lies about Maiden's absence from the flat.'

'And that's good enough?'

'It supports a charge.'

'But will it convict her?'

'In my opinion.'

Reason's stare was piercing. 'I have to be certain. If she could do it once, she could do it again.'

'No, no!' Welles burst out. 'You can't turn against her like this, Charles. She may have acted the fool, but she isn't bad, and I'll never believe she meant harm to Ginny.'

Reason snarled: 'So what did she mean?'

'Who knows what went on in her silly brain? Some practical joke, anything. But she never expected it to end in murder.'

'You poor dupe.'

'Yes – anything!' Welles clasped his hands as if in prayer. 'But at the worst you can't go through with it – you can't do this to your own daughter.' He turned to me. 'Maiden is dead. Won't that do, without locking her away for twenty years?'

I said: 'She has a case to answer. Good or bad, a court will decide.'

'But she couldn't have known what the fellow would do – she may only have meant to scare poor Ginny! Believe me, she isn't really bad. Wilful and proud perhaps, but underneath there's a sensitive person. And a trial – no, you can't condemn her to that! Not to years wasted in prison. She couldn't stand it – oh, please! If there's a grain of humanity left in the law.'

I said: 'I'm sorry. But she must answer.'

'No – take me. Take me instead!'

I shook my head.

'But . . . with all that evidence?'

I simply shook my head again.

'Then . . . I'll fight it. I'll get the best counsel. I'll spend every last penny I've got.'

'That's your privilege.'

'Freddy-boy, Freddy, don't be a fool,' DeWitt said. 'She's got it coming.'

'Livvy is innocent!'

'Face it, old pardner. She's had you on a string.'

'I know her. I'll never believe it. She's my wife. She's my Livvy.'

DeWitt began to say something else, but was interrupted by a tap on the door. Pyatt entered. He glanced apprehensively at the company, and then at me. He said:

'Perhaps . . . a word outside, sir?'

'Livvy – you've got her here?' Welles exclaimed.

'If you don't mind, sir . . .'

'I demand to see her! She's my wife – you can't refuse.'

'Sir . . . ?'

I said: 'Is there a problem?'

But Welles had seized hold of Pyatt's arm. 'My wife – my wife! Where is she?'

After a moment, Pyatt blurted: 'I'm afraid she's dead, sir.'

'Dead!'

'I'm sorry, sir.' Pyatt tried to retrieve his arm, but failed. Welles was gazing at him dementedly, but no more so than Charles Reason.

'Dead!'

'Yes sir.'

'But she can't be – you're talking of Garry Maiden!'

'Hell, oh hell,' DeWitt groaned. 'Not another.'

'She can't be dead!'

'Yes sir.'

'No. Oh no!'

I snapped: 'How did it happen?' Pyatt got his arm back at last, and massaged it feelingly. He said:

'A bit of a cock-up, sir, I'm afraid. But the girl couldn't have known what she would do.'

'The girl?'

'One of the WPCs. Mrs Welles wanted to know if chummie Maiden had got away. So this girl let slip what happened to him, and then the lady went berserk. She ran through to the kitchen and bolted the door, and by the time we'd got it open it was too late.'

'Well?'

'Used a chef's knife, sir. Dead before the ambulance got there.'

Reason gave a great howl and dropped down on a chair: DeWitt helped the shaking Welles to another. Big-eyed, Susan Strickland stood gazing at her collapsed brother-in-law. Then she ran to him, sought to clasp him in an embrace.

'It's all right, Freddy, it's all right!'

Feebly he tried to push her away, but she hugged him tighter yet.

'It's all right, don't you see? She played you false from the start. Always. She boasted about it. Even on that honeymoon in Bermuda. And now she's gone, and you're free, and I'm here who's always loved you. So it's all right, it's how it should be, everything is working out right!'

'You – heartless – bitch!' He struggled, freed himself and sent her flying. He gasped: 'I hate you, Suzy-Lu! I never want to see your face again.'

Her scream was explosive. She threw herself on him. DeWitt grabbed her, she threw herself on DeWitt. I shouted: 'Get some women in here!' – and three WPCs hustled in, already alerted by the scream. They were barely enough. She screamed, kicked, punched, tore the hair of the unlucky officers, and, when finally overcome, went on screaming without intermission.

'Take her somewhere she can't be heard!'

They had to carry her out bodily, and there was no cessation of the screaming, though by degrees it died away. Reason howled:

'No more children! From this day let fatherhood be cursed.'

'Never, never!' Welles shouted after her, before collapsing again on a chair.

'Oh sweet, sweet Jesus!' DeWitt exclaimed. 'Is there going to be no end to this? I came here to collect the body of a wife, and all the time it gets worse. Is this where it stops, Gently?'

I said: 'They need someone to stand by them.'

'Sure, sure. To stand by them. But who in hell is going to stand by me?' He shook himself like a dripping retriever. 'So I get them out of here,' he said. 'Some place. God knows where. But out of here. Away from the cop-shop. Where shall it be, brother Frederick?'

'Oh Lord, not Eversley Square,' Welles groaned.

'Best a hotel, then. What have we got?'

Welles shuddered. 'Not Bertie's!'

'Give me that goddamn telephone.'

He rang the Hilton; and the Hilton obliged. Tanner sent Pyatt to call them a cab. Reason had slipped into a stupor again, and needed to be guided out to the transport. DeWitt gave me a quick, transatlantic handclasp; Welles thought about it, but didn't. I watched them go, then returned to the office, where I found Tanner lighting a mean cheroot. I said:

'It's your pigeon now.'

'Not tonight, sir,' Tanner said. 'Tonight, with no disres-pect, this effing police force can stick itself up its own backside. I'm knackered. I've had enough. I've got bad thoughts about the human race. Me and millionaires don't mix. So I'm going home to the wife and kids.'

It seemed a good idea. 'How many have you got?'

'Just the two, sir. Chris and Donna. He's eleven, she's thirteen, and she's growing up quite a looker.'

I kept the idea in mind as I collected the Rover and blew. Reason's Mini was still parked out front, but I doubted if a ticket or two would bother him.

12

That was five days before the hurricane and eight before the stockmarket crash. The first presented me with other involvements, the second, thanks to Reason, I could view with some detachment. I cannot, of course, make a positive connection between Reason's wild threats and Black Monday, and it may or may not be significant that computer-trading was a critical element in the event. I would merely point out that his large holdings were principally managed by this technique, and that on Wall Street the firm of Oppenheimer-DeWitt was ninety percent liquid on October 19th. While, as a bonus, and for some while after, I enjoyed almost the status of God with my stockbroker.

But of Reason we saw no more. He never returned to the flat in Lime Walk. The Coroner's Court returned appropriate verdicts, and presumably the old man buried his dead, while the grape-vine told me that Mrs Strickland had been referred to an institution that also boasted of a royal patient. In November, Gabrielle reported that a van had collected the bank of computers from the flat, and before Christmas there had moved in a retired clergyman by the name of Haliburton. One other odd happening that occurred at this time: a perfect snowstorm of anonymous donations. Cheques for one million pounds apiece descended on bewildered but delighted charities. There were many theories. Her Majesty's Opposition suspected a sly move by Chancellor Lawson. But by December, when the snowstorm ceased, no positive contender had been found. And Charles Sinjohn Reason seemed to have vanished from human ken.

But not quite.

On the following August, on a perfect afternoon at Heatherings, when the rolling fields of ling beyond our garden gate were shimmering with blueness and scent you could cut, the telephone rang. Gabrielle took it.

'My dear, it is the good Superintendent Sinclair who we met in Scotland. This is not business, he says, but a little matter with which you may help him.'

I took the phone. 'Gently here.'

'Ach, man! I'm sorry to be troubling you at home on the Sabbath. But I've got this mannie after buying my old car, and I'm not so dooms certain I should take a cheque from him. By his looks he's an old beggarman off the roads, but he claims to know you and says you'll give him a reference.'

'What's his name?'

'It is Charles Reason.'

'Reason!'

'Do you ken him, man?'

'Around seventy, five-ten, grey elf-locks?'

'That's a pairfect description of the mannie.'

'Yes,' I said. 'Yes, I ken him. And I think you might risk taking his cheque.'

'It's for fifteen hundred pund, man!'

'Still, I think you can rest easy at night.' Then, after a pause, I added: 'But what's he doing in Dornoch?'

'That you may well be asking, man. He drew up this way in the spring, and moved into a croft cottage out in the hills. But devil a bit, he had the phone put on there, which must have cost a pretty penny – unless it is the

174

Hydro-Electric's doing, and they are casting eyes in that direction.'

'And he lives there alone – in the grey hills?'

'Ach, no! He's married Did you no ken?'

'Married!'

'Aye. To a wee Scots lassie who is young enough to be his grand-daughter. Lettie MacAndrew she used to be, the bairn of one of my officers. And whist! The rumour is that she's expecting a bairn of her own.'

I said: 'Pass on my regards and my admiration.'

'And I'll be for taking his cheque?'

'Ach, yes!'

'You did not mind me asking?. For the truth is he does not look worth a brass ha'peny.'

I hung up and told Gabrielle the news. She spent a long time staring at the sunny garden. Then she said:

'I am wondering, my friend. Will he be hoping for a girl – or for a boy?'

In due course I rang Sinclair in Sutherland. The wee Scots lassie had produced a son. He was born at New Year, and, strangely, it was then that Footsie – the Financial Times-Stock Exchange Index – at last got off its backside and began to motor.

Ah well. *C'est la vie.*

[Brundall, 1988/89]

NOTE I have to offer further acknowledgements to our old Warwickshire colleague, who also used this theme. Rather well.

AH